INDIAN CHARGE

The Indians were waiting.

They had hidden in a thicket and must have watched me from the time I topped the swell above the valley. They both carried rifles.

Before I could react, I saw a puff of blue smoke and saw one of the Indians charge through it. A great fist from nowhere hit me in the midsection, and the world slanted crazily. Reflexes took over. I somehow raised my rifle and aimed the muzzle at the charging savage, now only a few yards away.

I fired.

A riderless painted pony veered past me. But by now my horse was pitching wildly and I was half out of the saddle. My coordination was all wrong, and a terrible ache was spreading across my belly. And that's when the second Indian came for me. . . .

BEST OF THE WEST
from Zebra Books

BROTHER WOLF (1728, $2.95)
by Dan Parkinson
Only two men could help Lattimer run down the sheriff's killers—a stranger named Stillwell and an Apache who was as deadly with a Colt as he was with a knife. One of them would see justice done—from the muzzle of a six-gun.

CALAMITY TRAIL (1663, $2.95)
by Dan Parkinson
Charles Henry Clayton fled to the west to make his fortune, get married and settle down to a peaceful life. But the situation demanded that he strap on a six-gun and ride toward a showdown of gunpowder and blood that would send him galloping off to either death or glory on the . . . *Calamity Trail*.

THUNDERLAND (1991, $3.50)
by Dan Parkinson
Men were suddenly dying all around Jonathan, and he needed to know why—before he became the next bloody victim of the ancient sword that would shape the future of the Texas frontier.

APACHE GOLD (1899, $2.95)
by Mark K. Roberts & Patrick E. Andrews
Chief Halcon burned with a fierce hatred for the pony soldiers that rode from Fort Dawson, and vowed to take the scalp of every round-eye in the territory. Sergeant O'Callan must ride to glory or death for peace on the new frontier.

OKLAHOMA SHOWDOWN (1961, $2.25)
by Patrick E. Andrews
When Dace chose the code of lawman over an old friendship, he knew he might have to use his Colt .45 to back up his choice. Because a meeting between good friends who'd ended up on different sides of the law as sure to be one blazing hellfire.

Available wherever paperbacks are sold, or order direct from the Publisher. Send cover price plus 50¢ per copy for mailing and handling to Zebra Books, Dept. 1549, 475 Park Avenue South, New York, N.Y. 10016. Residents of New York, New Jersey and Pennsylvania must include sales tax. DO NOT SEND CASH.

BLOOD ARROW

BY

DAN PARKINSON

ZEBRA BOOKS
KENSINGTON PUBLISHING CORP.

ZEBRA BOOKS

are published by

Kensington Publishing Corp.
475 Park Avenue South
New York, NY 10016

Second printing: July 1987

Printed in the United States of America

for Carol

Chapter One

Captain Mellett had left the Murphy brothers to watch the pack horses and extra saddle mounts in a high-walled park near the base camp when we set out to explore the peaks to the south. But he began to worry about them when we found Indian sign a few miles out. And when we found traces of a large party, he decided to regroup. So he sent two of us, Billy Le-Croix and me, back to get them.

The captain and Pastor Goodwin had felt sure we were alone in this great region, beyond the normal range of the known tribes. But evidence of savages about changed that. Now we had to keep together and be prepared for anything. So we were about in the dark hours of a crystal cold morning, full of coffee and biscuits, and saddled for a fast ride north. Old Rollo packed biscuits and jerky for us, and the captain laid a hand on both our shoulders. "You watch your back trail, boys," he said. "We will look for you at nightfall."

We rode out then, through a shadowed cleft into high mountain country, bathed in silver moonlight. A mile or more out, Billy drew rein below a pinnacle of rock and held up his hand. We sat for a time listening. There was nothing but the living silence of the mountains. Finally he said, "Thought I heard something," and we moved on.

We were the youngest among Captain Mellett's expedition, Billy being just twenty and I a few months younger. But we had carried our full weight from the outset and sometimes more, looking to the time when we would set winter camp and share in the proceeds of a season's trapping. There were twenty-two in the expedition who came to the Shining Mountains seeking prime winter plew.

If Captain Mellett was a fool, as some claimed, he was a glorious fool, and there was a pride in following him. From his own purse he had outfitted us all and led us west. His detractors were now far behind us. A few at Independence had belittled the thought of following Zebulon Pike's route, favoring the more recent trail of Bonneville and Bridger. We would border Spanish lands, they said, too far south for the best pelts and too removed from the fur rendezvous for trading. But the captain was resolved, and we were with him to a man.

The march westward, at first by wagon trail and then, leaving that, across awesome plains and into the land of rolls and breaks that presaged the first view of the barrier mountains, had toughened us and honed our senses, but we had lost neither man nor beast enroute. The plains we crossed were home to the Kiowa, but we saw none. Not until we came into the broken lands, in fact, did we see wild Indians, and then but few. There was a group of five or six who watched us from a distance and followed us the better part of a day before turning away.

There was also the little band we met in a valley below the foothills. Beside a stream, sheltered by cottonwoods, they had set a smoke-darkened tipi and erected a sort of lean-to of sticks and grass. We rode up on them, topping a ridge just above their camp. I was

8

among those in the lead and thought I counted several forms darting for cover at sight of us. But when we came closer there was only one, an old man leaning on a stick and holding up his hand to us in sign of peace.

We meant no harm and wanted none, so we held back while the captain and old Rollo rode forward to talk with him. They were down there for what seemed a long time, the captain and Rollo sitting in their saddles, the old Indian leaning on his stick before them, his hands speaking. Rollo occasionally responded, his hands moving easily in the sign, and he would now and then turn to Captain Mellett, interpreting. When the talking was done, they returned. We left a pack of meal and salt and a little dried meat, then circled the camp and went on our way.

They were waifs—an old man, two women, and a child—the remains of a village which had stood a few miles downstream. Men had ridden into their village with guns, killing many, scattering the rest. These had slipped away and were waiting now for other survivors, if any, to rejoin them.

Their attackers had been white men. "Renegades, most likely," the captain had said, and we kept a closer watch at night after that until we were into the mountains.

There was something else the old man had said, about it being a bad time, a time of change. There was pressure from the north, and tribes were moving, shifting their hunting grounds, each pressing in upon some neighbor. Unsettled times, Rollo had said.

And I thought of this now as Billy LeCroix and I rode northward through the hours of dark and dawn. Where we were—inside the east range of the mountains, far from the Cheyenne, past the Arapahoe, and far north of the Comanche—there should be no tribes and few hunting parties. Captain Mellett had read much and chosen carefully. But there were Indians. We had found sign of several parties — or one large party — within a few miles. I carried the fine rifle Captain Mellett had issued me, and I checked it again as we rode.

First light, that sudden redefinition of the landscape which comes without warning in the mountains, found us far north of our company, riding into a wide valley where tall silver grass eased down toward a rushing stream sounding among stands of spruce and juniper. Beyond and above, a ridge cloaked in yellow aspen awaited the kiss of the morning sun.

At the stream we turned aside to enter a copse where we could rest out of sight, and climbed down to let our horses drink. We stamped around, blew into our hands, and flapped our arms to relieve the numbing of the cold.

Billy stepped to the thicket's edge and looked back the way we had come, then swore an oath. "Fine pair of mountain men we are," he sneered. "Look at that, Randy. Just look."

I looked. Where we had ridden down the long grass slope was a trail a blind man could have followed, a long, plain swatch of green through the dew-silvered grass.

"If redskins are anywhere about," Billy observed, "we could be in a good bit of trouble, at least until the sun cures that pasture."

We wasted no time in moving out. If Will Farris and old Rollo had taught us nothing else on this expedition, they had taught us not to leave clear trail in hostile country. We heeled our mounts into the shallow stream and rode a half mile with it before climbing the other bank. From the top of the far ridge an hour later we looked back over the valley, studying the way we had come. The trail through the wet grass was still dimly visible, but there was no sign of any pursuit.

With the sunrise, brilliant red across the teeth of the eastern range, we paused again to survey the panorama around us. A sparred peak beyond us blazed red and gold, its fire echoed by other peaks beyond, each thrusting above its own solemn valleys where morning had not yet come. And I thought there could be no finer thing than to be alive in this fantastic land on this bright morning, a man in a man's place. From a crag southwest of us an eagle spiraled high into the sunlight on flashing wings.

Watching the eagle soaring overhead, I thought back on the day I had left my uncle's house to join Captain Mellett. Until then, my eyes had not been accustomed to focusing on anything more vast that the cold walls of a garret room or the dingy, mud-spattered streets of a town. But now, I was free, a man in a man's world. From where I sat, the lost, warm years of childhood were a dim memory while the later years in the academy were like sharp recollections of another person in another time. And those more recent memories, the death of my parents, the abrupt end of my schooling, the cold bed and hard work in my uncle's house, held no regret.

I was to have been, had my parents survived and had I achieved it, a man of letters, and thus, possibly, a man of means. It was their desire that I, their only child, might in some way gain eminence, though in honesty, I must admit, the desire had been more theirs than mine. They had sent me to Springfield, to the academy, and there maintained my tuition and board. And although I had never been of a scholarly bent, it was a bright and pleasant time in memory. It ended in my seventeenth year.

It was a season of fever, and my mother was ill. I was on my way home to Freeport the day my father stum-

11

bled in the rutted street and fell beneath a freight wagon. My mother survived him by only a week. My father's estate, his debts and his son were taken over by his brother in Independence.

My uncle was a stern, penurious man with little use for scholarly pursuits, and less for an overgrown nephew. He let me a bed in his house and place at his table, and hired me out to those who could pay for the cutting of wood, the tilling of fields, and the cleaning of barns. The day Captain Mellett arrived in Springfield to announce in the town square that he was making up a furring brigade for the Shining Mountains I was there and heard him. After I finished that day's work, I sought him out and signed his log. From that day I did not sleep again at my uncle's house.

"Come on, dreamer," Billy said. "It's time we moved on."

Billy's voice gave me a start and brought me back to the situation at hand. Rifles on saddlebows, we headed downslope. Across the valley, miles ahead but seeming nearer, was the crest of that flat rim that marked the walled meadow where the pack and saddle herd grazed. As we left the ridgetop I thought I heard a sound behind us, dim and far away, a quick drumming sound, and then it was whisked away as a vague breeze shifted. But when I paused and listened, there was nothing.

The autumn sun stood high and warm when we came into the meadow. The horses were there, grazing on ripe grass, but there was no sign of the Murphy brothers.

"They've gone off somewhere," Billy mused. We looked around a bit, then circled the meadow and finally split up and searched the surrounding rocks and the slopes and shoulders beyond, but we could find no sign of them.

"Captain's gonna give them some hell," Billy said, and I agreed. Neither of the Murphys had ever struck me as exceptionally bright, but they were steady and hard-working men well into their twenties, and it was unlike them to go shirking off when there was a job to do. And the captain was expecting us to be back by nightfall.

"They'll be back in a bit," I said. Billy was counting the stock.

"I make it two missing," he said. "They've ridden off to shoot meat, I wager. We can wait a bit."

We gathered the herd into a little box canyon near where we had brush-plugged the meadow's only easy gap, then sat down to rest and eat.

After a while Billy asked me, "What will you do with your share, Randy?"

I had given thought to the wealth a good winter's trapping would bring—my share alone could be several hundred dollars. But before I could answer he said, "I know what I will do with mine. I'll go back to Lane's Ferry and buy a farm. And I will marry."

"Do you know who will marry you?"

"Of course I know. Didn't I tell you? She's the daughter of the man who keeps the mercantile, and when I come home, we will be married."

He drew himself up a little and added with pride. "I have called on her at her home."

"There was a girl in Independence," I said, "at the boarding house just down the street. Her mother kept the house, and—"

"Her name is Sarah," Billy continued, not hearing a word I said. "She has hair like the gold in a coin, and eyes just the shade of that sky off there where the dark peaks are. And she's tall, near as tall as me. . . ."

He was off, with the bit in his teeth, so I sat back and listened, and that dark-haired girl in Independence, who tended to be a bit sharp around the edges anyway, gave way in my mind to a fair-haired girl a man could call his own. Not just like Billy's Sarah, maybe not so tall or so

13

prim as the vision he described, maybe a bit smaller and softer, but no matter. He talked on, and then neither of us talked; we just sat and thought our thoughts.

It was an hour, I suppose, before we roused ourselves, and still no sign of the Murphys. There was nothing else for it, and the stock was getting restless in the confined canyon. Finally, we built a small cairn of stones, pointing back to the south, and saddled up. I changed horses, saddling a stout roan that I particularly liked. Grouping the pack animals on leads, letting the saddle stock move free, we drove out of the meadow and pointed back the way we had come, to where Captain Mellett's camp lay beyond a distant ridge and a hot meal would be waiting that evening.

We recrossed the finger ridge a bit west of where we had crossed coming out, and headed down to the valley stream at a point near where we had stopped that morning. The dew trail we had left in the morning hours had been worrying us both, so going up that slope we were more alert than ever, and we found our previous tracks. They were there, right where we had left them. And there were others.

Two unshod horses had passed the spot sometime after us, moving north, one on each side of the faint remains of our own trail. I held the herd while Billy rode back down toward the stream, his rifle at the ready. He was gone for a while, and when he came back he was worried.

"Those were Indian ponies. They followed our track to the creek. I don't know where they went from there."

Since entering the mountains we had seen no redmen, nor should any be in this region. But some were, and they knew of us, and we didn't know where they were now. The little knot of worry that had ridden with me since morning was becoming very noticeable. Still, there was no further sign of life. We lined the herd out and

14

pushed them with renewed speed back toward the last ridge beyond which, a few miles away in a boulder-strewn canyon, lay friends and safety.

The sun was going down as we topped out and pointed the herd down toward the shadowed depth below. In the distance, we could see the cluster of rock we had departed in the early hours of morning, and I asked Billy, calling back over my shoulder, "Shouldn't there be smoke there?"

Oddly, it seemed, there was none.

We reached the valley floor some ways below the campsite and turned the herd through a narrow cleft that broadened slowly toward the campsite. Ahead was silence.

Suddenly the lead animals slowed, their ears up. One shied toward a near bank, the others around him following. In a moment they were huddled, skittish as colts on a lead, snorting, pawing, and facing ahead. There was a shoulder of rock there, and as we rounded it the roan shied and almost threw me off. I got him under control and looked down. A man lay there, dead.

It was Rowan Spring, big easygoing Rowan of the ready tongue. He lay facedown, a broken shaft protruding from his side. The top of his head was a mat of dark, drying blood. Just beyond lay Farris and another man, one fallen over the other. A few feet away another man, unrecognizable, lay beneath a fallen horse. And old Rollo was sprawled against the rock bank, half upright, dead eyes staring at the sky.

At a sound behind me I looked around. Billy was off his horse and sick. I thought I might be sick later, but now I was simply stunned. In a daze I stared about me at the remains of the Mellett expedition.

Captain Mellett had died beside a great jagged stone, four gaping lance wounds in his body. Young Jarod Branch had been crushed beneath a horse's hoofs. Ben

Foley lay at the base of a rock where he had fallen, his neck broken by a war club's impact. Each bore the mark of the vanquished — blood and bone where their hair should have been.

Suddenly I became aware that I could barely see them, and I shook myself and looked around. It had grown dark while I stood there. Down the canyon the horses we had brought milled and shuffled, dissatisfied with where they were, afraid to venture away. By the far wall of the canyon I found Billy, sitting as though in a trance, facing away from the carnage about us.

Eventually I found some twigs and branches and got a small fire going on a ledge above the ruined campsite, as far as possible from the scene just below. Billy crawled up to join me, dragging his rifle behind him.

"They are killed," he said. His voice was faraway.

"Yes."

"All of them. They are dead."

"Yes."

"My dear God," he breathed and sat down abruptly on a rock.

It was full dark when we finally gathered in the horses, leading them out of the canyon to a broad shelf above our ledge, away from the smell of death.

Then we slept.

Chapter Two

On a grey morning we did what needed to be done.

In a cache behind some rock, we found a portion of the expedition's supplies, overlooked by the savages. There were a few tools, some foodstuffs, and a good supply of powder and ball. A leathern case held Captain Mellett's log, a few personal papers, and three well-thumbed books, one his Bible. Scattered around the camp were a few discarded things, among them three bales of traps. All of the horses were gone except for two that were dead, and of course all the weapons had been taken.

We went among the bodies, identifying them as best we could while I wrote their names in Captain Mellett's log. There were seventeen. We never found Pastor Goodwin. Two axes and a sturdy spade were among the rubble. But nothing we found would break the flinty ground of the place. Finally we dragged all the bodies to a rockfall sloping from the canyon wall and labored to cover them over with bits of stone. It was the best grave we could devise.

Billy brought up the captain's Bible, and I read some words over them as morning sunlight found the canyon floor. Finally, I entered in the log a description of the place where the expedition had ended. We signed it, William J. LeCroix and Randall Kerry, then closed the book and sealed it.

"When we get home," I told Billy, "we must find the captain's heirs and deliver this book and the captain's horses to them." I was still muddled in my mind, and knew it, but somehow the idea became a thing to hold onto. It made sense, and in making sense, it was superior to any other perception I was capable of at the moment. The idea took root as I said it and became the most important thing in my mind.

Billy glanced at me as though I had gone daft but said nothing. We stood there, looking around us at the serrated canyon walls and beyond, unseen, the expanse of the wilderness in which we were alone.

"Billy, we'd best be away from here—somewhere we can rest and think."

I believe at that moment the magnitude of our situation hit both of us, and we hurried to pack what we could find and gathered the horses. There was in this land one place familiar to us, and we turned toward it, north, toward the meadow where the horses had been kept. There, or somewhere in between, we might find the Murphy brothers. I counted on it. There was no one else in this wide mountain world to look for.

We had gone a mile when Billy drew up and turned, his face drained of color. "Randy, the Indians—those two that followed us—"

I hadn't forgotten them, but his mention brought upon me something I had not felt until now: an anger that settled into my numbed mind and took hold. I couldn't accept the atrocity we had left behind us. I wanted to strike out at something. It was a hunger, and its pangs drew me up in the saddle.

"If we find them," I told him, "we will kill them."

I was again riding the spirited roan, and Billy, a black. Four of the spare horses carried packs. The air was sharp and clear with a feel of frost about it. Old Rollo had warned that winter came suddenly in this land, and I reckoned it would come soon.

Atop the crest heading that broad, sloping meadow which sprawled down toward the little stream, we ranged both directions looking for tracks but found none. The grass slope spread before us, unblemished and silver-green in the bright sunlight. Satisfied, we headed down toward the creek nearly a mile away.

The Indians were waiting for us there.

They had hidden in a thicket and must have watched us from the time we topped the swell above the valley. We were nearly down when they showed themselves. They rode out of the trees, arrogant and sure, and faced us from a hundred yards away.

The first was a magnificent savage in full array, his broad face streaked with paint, buckskin shirt glistening with clusters of beads. The second was smaller and less gaudy. Both carried rifles.

At the sight of them, I wheeled the roan as the hackles rose on my neck, and Billy's mount blundered into me from behind before sidestepping away. Then we sat, for a long moment, staring across the intervening grass at them and they at us.

It came with terrifying suddenness. The feathered warrior said something and gestured. The second one looked at him for an instant, then at us. There was that instant's hesitation, then he heeled his mount and whipped forward, low over the animal's neck, straight at us like a bolt from a string, raising his rifle as he came.

I saw the puff of blue smoke and saw him charge through it. A great fist from nowhere hit me in the midsection, and the world slanted crazily. Reflexes took over, and I noticed, from some great distance, that my rifle was up and its sights bore on the charging savage, now only a few yards away, and I fired.

A riderless painted pony veered past me, and as Billy shouted something I saw the Indian hit the ground. I realized in a dull fashion that my horse was pitching wildly and that I was half out of the saddle. With difficulty, I drew myself back up. My coordination was all wrong, and a terrible ache was spreading across my belly.

The big warrior still sat his horse where they had first appeared, and now he raised his rifle, methodically, and took aim. Billy was a few feet away, rifle still across his saddlebow, staring stupidly at me. I pointed and shouted, and he came to his senses. But his reaction was slow and uncoordinated. I knew as his rifle rose that he would miss.

The warrior didn't miss. Both rifles sounded and Billy pitched backward off his saddle, landing in a heap on the hard ground. Across the grass the Indian lowered his smoking gun and, leaning far down, laid it gently on the ground. He straightened again, lifted a long hatchet from his belt, and grinned at me.

In those frenzied seconds my mind had clouded, a welter of pain and confusion that stifled every other feeling. But now, seeing the grin on that painted face as I sat dazed with an empty gun and an aching belly, something terrible broke loose inside me. All the loss, the misery, and the awful loneliness of the past hours, the vision of friends lying dead, and the cold anger that had come of it, all achieved sudden focus now on that grinning heathen face, and a pure hatred blazed forth that shut out everything else. As he closed in, I let loose a war cry every bit as bloodthirsty as his own and spurred to meet him.

In the blink of an eye we met. The long hatchet whistled around and over in an arc toward my head, and I raised my rifle in both hands and went for his face with it, gripping it wide and pushing broadside at him. I felt the hatchet deflected, and the next instant the rifle caught him in the throat and he was gone, dropping away beneath me.

I was off my horse then, sprawled on the ground. I tried twice before getting my feet under me. A few feet away the beaded warrior was on one knee, hands at his face, trying to stand. In two strides I was beside him. Taking the long rifle by its muzzle I swung it full circle with all my strength, bringing it down across the back of his neck.

He was dead when his face hit the ground.

Still blinded by that terrible red anger, I drew my knife and raised the hair on his head, holding it with one hand while I cut deep around the topknot. A quick pull and I held the bleeding scalp aloft while a sweet, clear tide of vengeance swept over me. The moment was a savage, singing epitaph for all those good men back there in that rock canyon. It was a frozen instant of mindless, thundering glory.

A moment later I was sitting cross-legged on the ground, face buried in my hands. Drained, purged, and blank, I sat like that. My belly ached, I was sick through and through, and I had no inclination to move or even think. I just sat and shook. Eventually, it passed.

Awareness. Still shaking, I cleaned the broad knife and put it away. Then I pulled the rifle to me, and clumsily, slowly, reloaded it, getting to my feet as I did. The waves of pain in my belly were duller now, subsiding. I lifted my shirt. The ornate iron buckle on my leather belt was creased inward at a crazy slant. The skin beneath it was turning dark from the bruise.

The mutilated warrior lay at my feet. Off to the left Billy was as he had fallen, and I knew he had not lived to see the end of it. There was something Old Rollo had said one evening as we sat around a chip fire on the Great Plains. The quick and the mean. The quick survive on God's great mountains, and the mean prosper.

Oh, Billy. Why weren't you quicker—or meaner?

The horses had scattered over a quarter-mile of that broad pasture but were grazing now and beginning to drift back toward me. I turned to count them, and there was that second Indian, the one I had shot, up on his knees a few yards away and struggling to reload his rifle.

Fever-bright eyes burned at me from a dark face splotched with dirt and smudged paint. His buckskin shirt was matted with bright blood from shoulder to waist. I raised my rifle, and lowered it again. I simply had had enough of killing right then. I strode forward to where he crouched and kicked the gun from his hands. The force of it toppled him backward, and the strength was gone from him. He lay where he fell.

Folk may vary in the limits of their remorse. Mine, for the moment, was all used up. I mourned, in a way, Captain Mellett and his dream lying back there beneath a talus fall and Billy sprawled in death there in the grass, but it was a distant, far-off mourning, something set aside for a more placid time. Billy LeCroix had been too slow. He hadn't measured up. Somehow, when it counted, I had.

I brought in some of the horses and found the pack with the spade. I buried Billy in a shallow grave where he had fallen, and the mounded soil was lost among the flags of the grass. Then working on foot, I gathered in the horses, talking them in, calming them, and guiding them down into that safe thicket below. Circling the area, I gathered up the rifles—Billy's good Hawken, the big brave's French trade rifle, and the young Indian's old flintlock. I stripped the warrior's knife, belt, and flask from his body and picked up the long hatchet from where it lay.

The sun was low in the southwest, touching the far mountains, when I finished the chores I could find to do — all but one — and laid a small fire back under the trees at the creek's edge. Then I went once more out into the meadow. The young Indian was still there, lying where he had fallen, but still alive.

Running a belt around his shoulders, I dragged him back to the fire, then cut away the buckskin shirt. My ball had struck him high in the left side and had gone completely through, leaving a gaping wound in his back below the shoulder. It was ugly and had bled a great deal but was not spurting blood, and I found no sign of shattered bone.

He was barely conscious as I began cleaning his wounds, and passed out again when I seared the hole in his back with a hot knife blade. I salved and patched him, and cleaned his face to salve a stone-cut above his eyes. Oddly, without the war paint, he looked for a moment like a sick child, although I made him to be my age or a bit more. The illusion was shattered when he opened his eyes in a moment of awareness and glared at me with a malevolence no child could have produced.

I found a pot and heated a broth of meat and ground oats, which he accepted in half-consciousness when I spooned it into him. He ate a good measure of it, in fact, before gaining awareness again. Then suddenly his eyes flashed open, and he looked around, then at me, and spat porridge at my face.

And the anger was back. I jumped up, backed off a few steps, and cursed him roundly. I flung at him every insult I could call to mind, used every epithet I could think of, and thought seriously of slitting his heathen throat.

"Why don't you just go ahead and die!" I was shouting and couldn't have stopped if I'd wanted to. "You'd be a sight better than you are now. You're nothing but a godless heathen."

When I finally ran down, those black eyes were regarding me calmly, and, so help me, there was a smirk of evil delight on his dark face. After a moment of silence he summoned his strength visibly and drew a shuddering breath.

"And you," he said, his voice barely audible, "are a fool."

Chapter Three

The remark came as something of a shock.

What I knew about Indians was mostly secondhand. Those I had seen in the East were tame, placid creatures for the most part, skulking around the edges of civilization, living in the woods along the river or in the streets of town — or, occasionally, as when Captain Faulk brought his Delaware scouts to Independence, proud and aloof, standing apart from the people around them. At the academy I had heard a lecture delivered by an educated Delaware, a wizened old man whose name was Josiah Tree. Afterward there had been some spirited discussion among students as to whether Indians could be considered human. A few of the more serious souls held that they could, in some minor way, if they were Christian.

There had been a mission school for Pawnee, Pottawatomie, and Peoria youngsters at Bend Creek, near Independence, and I had seen some of those miserable little wretches being marched through town on occasion, a marm leading the way and a master coming behind with his switch. There were also Indians who spoke the white tongues, and some who could read, write, cipher, and recite. I had heard there was even a college in Illinois where they had a full-blood Cherokee as a professor.

But those weren't wild Indians. Nowhere along the way had I heard of a wild Indian speaking English. And it had never crossed my mind that one might. I didn't respond; I just stared as the little strength he had summoned receded from him, and he lay back, closing his eyes.

With nightfall it had turned colder, and I finally wrapped a blanket around my shoulders and moved close to the fire to finish off the bit of venison I had left. There was coffee, and I made it rich and black in a pan. It warmed me.

I found another blanket and covered the Indian. I managed to pour some coffee into him, though he was barely conscious now. And even as I did, I was wondering whether I shouldn't put him out of his misery. I was inclined to hate him, not comfort him, but I kept on tending him. I was, as he had said, a fool.

I could rationalize it, though. I could always dispatch him later, but curiosity demanded that I wait and see if he could indeed speak English. The idea made about as much sense as gathering horse eggs, but I was tired and defeated, lost and confused. And I simply didn't feel like killing that Indian right then.

There was the scalp I had taken, a grisly trophy of a moment of blind savagery that was at the same time repulsive and somehow exciting. The black hair was long and heavy and surprisingly clean. The flesh crown had begun to dry. I hung it back on my belt and huddled more closely by the fire.

A sound woke me.

It was dark, with the feel of early morning in the air. The fire was down to a few faint coals, and in the darkness the unconscious Indian was fighting for life. He had a raging fever and was breathing with visible effort.

I got the fire built up and put on more coffee. While it was making, I found two more blankets—one of which had been rolled behind the saddle of the warrior's horse—and covered him over with these. From coals I built two more fires, one one each side of him, and stretched pack canvas on limbs back of them to reflect the heat. With the coffee hot, I added handfuls of loaf sugar and worked for an hour or more, into the early dawn, getting as much of it into him as I could. I knew of nothing else to do.

He should have died that morning, but he didn't. By the time the sun was up, his breathing had eased. And as the chill was burned from the mountain air his fever broke, and he fell into a quiet sleep. I washed in the icy creek and tended the horses, bunched during the night and spreading now as they grazed. There were thirteen with the two Indian ponies, and these I worked with for a while, coaxing and gentling them to my touch.

I had no real plan for what to do next. In the back of my mind was the idea that the Murphy brothers would show up soon, from wherever they had gone, and I had best stay where they could find me. This was as good a spot as any, with wood and water at hand. And if they didn't show up? I wasn't ready to think about that possibility just yet.

The dead warrior lay where he had fallen, almost hidden in the tall grass—out on the sloping prairie. I was tempted to leave him there for the wolves, but finally got out the spade and went and covered him over with sod in a shallow grave. I didn't go again to the place where I had buried Billy.

Back at the creek I managed a breakfast of oat cakes and coffee, and a little later got an oat cake and more coffee into the Indian. He looked at me dully, got the food down and went back to sleep. He looked like he might heal, in time, but I couldn't really say I cared either way.

At mid-morning, I saddled the roan and headed upstream to find meat. I passed by rabbits, grouse, and the like several times, looking for something to provide more meat with less shooting. Several miles upstream, the creek's wide valley narrowed into a rocky gorge shadowed by high, vertical walls of red and mustard stone where dark cedars crested the clifftop above. Beyond this, past a long bend, was a wooded slope dark with patches of forest and laced with deadfall in a cove at its foot. There were deer just above the bend, but they spooked and disappeared before I could get a shot. I went on, half hunting, half simply enthralled with the unfolding landscapes that changed with every turn.

I paused partway up a long, wooded slope to rest the roan, then led the animal the rest of the way to the top. At the crest, the land fell away before me in a scene of fantastic beauty. Ahead and below was a wild valley quilted in the colors of talus slopes, dark pines, deadfall mazes, meadows, and red rock shoulders, threaded through by the stream's gorge which I had left. Beyond was a great, gentle swell, climbing away into blue distance, spanning outward and upward toward the base of a great stone slab, a misted monolith standing stark against the receding peak behind it.

Here and there a bird call sparkled the crystal stillness, echoed in hue by the flash of aspen stands scattered in the distance. Beyond the broken region that dark pine forest was like a royal carpet swelling to the foot of the ancient, regal rock. Humbler elevations to the right and left knelt before it as it stood there, serene in its piercing grandeur, God's altar in a cathedral of his own design.

For a long time I stood there, awed by the terrible

beauty spread before me. Never had I seen, nor could I have imagined, anything to compare with the immense court of that king among rocks.

The sun sat on the peak behind that monolith when I finally mounted and turned away, and the troubling idea was on me that I didn't want to leave this place. Somewhere, not yet discerned in my disordered thought, was another perspective to consider when I eventually got around to deciding what to do next.

Turning south I left the ridge and followed the next narrow valley downward to the east. I had gone less than half a mile when a fat doe broke from the underbrush and bounded up the slope just ahead. Rifle up, I "thought" the shot home and the animal pitched forward and lay still. I reloaded, then sat for a time surveying the surrounding skylines before continuing.

I took the quarters, the heart, and the liver of the animal, bound them in the hide, and headed back across the long swell beside me and downstream toward my camp. I stopped long enough to fill my hat with some redbrown berries which I had seen Old Rollo collect and cook into a tart pudding with a bit of flour. They were on a wide shelf above the creek bed on the north side, a shelf which widened and descended until it became part of the north rise of the valley further downstream.

Here, where the berries were, the shelf was high, and sitting my horse at the lip I could scan the width of the wide valley toward the south and east, my eyes above the level of the cottonwood trees along the stream. I made note of the place, to return here later if I needed to survey the valley for game without riding all over it.

It was not a friendly country, I thought as I started back toward camp, but it could be a pleasant country for a man unburdened and willing to accept it on its

29

terms.

Evening was upon the valley as I rode on down-stream. The chill in the high country air again carried a hint of coming winter. Soon I was going to have to think about the future.

I made a wide half circle around the campsite to come in from the far side, using a caution I was rapidly learning in these mountains, but found nothing amiss. The horses were still gathered in the near meadow, the campsite was well hidden among the trees, and I found no tracks which had not been there before. I was at once relieved and disappointed. All through the day, I had hoped the Murphys might be here when I returned.

The Indian had moved while I was gone. Somehow he had gotten down to the creek to drink, and he lay there now, just above the bank, exhausted and weak but awake.

After I had unsaddled and tended the roan, I built up the fire again, using tinder to blow the last coals back into flame, then cut up a quarter of the venison, speared chunks of it on willow branches, and set it over the flames to sear. I put on a pan of water for coffee. Then with the fire crackling steady and the flames subsided, I raised the meat to roast and set about inventorying the supplies and possessions at hand.

It was a peculiar legacy — thirteen horses, two saddles, four pack saddles, two Hawken rifles, a French short rifle, and an old flintlock, about sixty beaver traps, two axes and a spade, various small tools, and enough flour, salt, coffee, and meal to last at least a few weeks. Plus two good knives, two trade knives taken from the Indians — and there should have been a hatchet. It wasn't there.

I cocked my rifle and walked to where the Indian lay, half upright against a tree bole by the creek. "Give it up," I said, and brought the gun to bear. He didn't move a muscle, but those black eyes held mine. Where he sat, his right hand was out of sight, down by his leg.

For a long moment we remained like that, I with the rifle trained on him and he silently daring me to kill him, as though he had decided one of us was going to die, and he didn't particularly care which one. His eyes flickered for an instant to my belt, where the scalp of the other Indian still hung, and the muscles contracted in his shoulder. I tightened my finger on the trigger. But he should have been standing before me, not lying there half dead.

I backed off a few steps and lowered the hammer.

"You can go to the devil, heathen," I said. "You can sit there and starve for all of me."

I went back to the fire where the meat was sizzling and the water was boiling, and set about making my supper. I had thought a time or two during the day about throwing away the grisly trophy at my belt, but now I decided I would not. I would wear it with pride, and if the opportunity offered I would add companions to it.

I was, again, surprised at that Indian. By no means should he have been inclined—or able—to pose challenge to me at this point. He could no more swing that tomahawk than I could fly, but he intended to try if I let him. I gave it up. It was beyond understanding.

The meat was excellent and I was hungrier than I had thought. I ate two or three pounds of it and a brace of meal cakes washed down with steaming coffee before I was satisfied.

The horses gathered in toward the fire with the coming of darkness, and several of them drifted down to the creek, stepping gingerly past the Indian to get there. One of the pack animals wandered over to him and nuzzled him curiously. He managed to lift a hand and pat its muzzle, then sagged back again wearily.

It would have been a pleasant evening there at that campfire, in the high cool mountains—but for that Indian.

He lay over by the creek, wounded and hungry, and swathed in heathen righteousness, his existence a discordant note. He had wrapped himself in idiotic pride, and I was not about to try again to help him.

Nearly an hour had passed before I heard a thump and looked up to see the hatchet scudding across the ground to the base of the tree where the packs were hung. I went and got it and set it high in the tree, then took the deer liver from the hide pouch and spread it on willow boughs over the glowing coals of the fire. I moved the coffee in close.

Then I went to the Indian and dragged him back to the fireside to have his supper.

Chapter Four

His name was Han-Ra-Hay. He chose to be a
mountain Ute. That is, he was born a Pawnee Indian
in the Missouri Plains but didn't stay that way. Like
me, he had been orphaned, but at an early age. A
hungry waif in a shabby village on the fringes of white
civilization, he had been delivered up to the tribe's
white agent for care.

"I was raised around the white-eyes," he said, hurting some but resting easy. "Went to agency school,
played 'little Indian boy' for the paleface trade, 'til I
was big enough to start getting whipped every Satur-
day by the town boys, and finally got big enough to do
some whipping of my own.

"I kept track, and when I got ready, I took them one
at a time and settled scores. Then I lit a shuck. Picked
up a horse that wasn't being used and went west to
join the free people."

Alone, on a stolen horse, he had traveled six hundred miles through a hostile land before finding a village of mountain Utes. That was two years ago. I
gathered it had taken a while for him to become more
than an accepted alien among the wild people, and
somehow I got the impression he had never quite
made it, though he had tried.

The tribe was that of Hotumin and Quanas. Hotumin, chief in council, was an aging leader who had led the tribe well for many seasons among the high mountains to the north and west, occupying at will a whole series of rich valleys where food was abundant and enemies few. Then others had come—Han-Ra-Hay was not definite about who they were—and the tribe was pressed further and further back, into these mountains finally, and those to the west. And Quanas became leader. Quanas the war chief.

Han-Ra-Hay got his name—and a measure of acceptance—from Quanas. The Pawnee had led a group of three young Utes in an impromptu raid on a hunting party of "the others" and brought back horses.

"Quanas himself called me Han-Ra-Hay," he said with pride, "and he told me to ride for a while with Uinay, the scout."

This had been his first legitimate raid with a war party. Quanas and a large band had come east, across high country, for a fall raid out of the mountains for horses and plunder. They had stumbled across our expedition and might have just looked them over and passed on by. But someone in the company had panicked and opened fire.

"So Quanas killed them," he said matter-of-factly. "Took the horses and guns. Uinay and me, we watched from a hill, and when the sun was high we found your trail and followed."

It was Uinay's scalp I wore at my belt now, and this Indian didn't like it.

"Uinay was a fine warrior, white-eyes. You were only lucky. His hair does you too much honor. You will not keep it long, or your own either. I said before, you are a fool."

Calmly, without blinking an eye, he told me I would die soon and that he would take my horses. The way he said it, it was a simple fact, hardly worth mentioning. And it angered me because it might be true.

"Well, Henry," I began in the most contemptous manner I could summon, and his eyes flashed malevolence.

"My name is Han-Ra-Hay, white-eyes. Cat of the Mountain!"

He tried to shout it but did not have the strength.

I felt no sympathy at all. "I care not a whit what you call yourself, Henry, you stinking aborigine. But it looks to me like, between us here, you are the one who's near to dying, not me. I have friends coming, and when they arrive we will deal with you or leave you. I don't really care which."

He looked puzzled for a moment, then thoughtful.

"Friends?" he asked. "Two white men?"

The way he said it, the hackles rose on my neck. I knew what came next, and I didn't want to hear it. I felt it would be the truth.

"Your friends won't be coming, white-eyes."

He saw my sudden confusion, grinned, and would say no more.

Two days later the Indian was still alive, the venison had run out and the Murphys had not come. So I went off to hunt again. I saddled Billy's black this time, and he tried his best to throw me before he accepted that I would ride him.

The horses were doing well on the lush green of the mountain slope but ranging out further than I liked, so I moved them into a grassed clearing above and closer to the camp. They could fatten on this valley graze in time, but time was becoming a problem.

Somewhere along there I decided it was best not to strike out for the east now, with winter coming on. When the cold winds came, it would be better in the mountain country than out on those endless, hostile plains. Somewhere south, I knew, was Santa Fe. But there were high passes between, and those high peaks already had snow growing on them.

The problem was the horses. I could have taken a saddle mount and pack horse and gone anywhere the impulse took me. But those horses were the last remains of Captain Mellett's expedition, and I didn't intend to lose them. The determination to hold and deliver the captain's stock and journal had become fixed in my mind and was important now beyond all reason.

So, the immediate problem was the immediate future. Food first, then a better place to stay. The creeksite camp was comfortable but exposed to the elements and to any enemies who happened along. It was visible and indefensible. I had to move, and soon.

Heading north this time, Han-Ra-Hay's cryptic statement about my friends not coming was much on my mind, and as I rode, I pointed back toward that walled meadow where I had last seen the Murphys. Vaguely, I was also looking for a place to take the horses, a place safe, where raiding parties might not see them and where drifting winds could not scatter them. I was thinking of the walled meadow that had been the captain's base.

But studying it after arriving there, I was not satisfied. It was a natural fort, high and clear of view around the caprock rim, an excellent headquarters for a strong, well-armed group. But for one man alone? I didn't think so. Its strength then would be a weakness. It was too obvious. It was not a place to hide; it was a place to defend.

What I needed was a hole somewhere, where a herd of horses might go unobserved. Unbidden, the great cathedral rock I had seen came to mind. I couldn't remember anything about it that offered hope for me, but I wanted to see it again. So I headed west and south in an arc that would take me that way. It was just a mile out, or less, that I found the tracks.

There was a broad, ravaged cutout where an earlier flood had washed across a little streamside park, baring the thin topsoil here and there. Clearly, in the whitish stuff between tufts of new weed, was the mark of a shod horse. And over there was another. Slowly, carefully, as Will Farris had taught me, I worked it out. There were a lot of tracks.

Two riders had entered the area from the east, the way I had come. Another, larger group had entered from the north. Where they had met and talked the tracks were thick. And from that point all of them, apparently had proceeded south or southeast. Beyond was rock and I could find no more sign. It was a puzzle. The two might have been the Murphy brothers. But what about the rest?

There was no answer to it here. I continued west.

Topping a high shoulder far north of the great rock, I looked out across vastness and could again see it, this time from a new angle. Again, off in the distance, it was an awesome thing. But though I looked at it for several minutes I saw no indication that it offered anything for me. From here I could tell that it was an enormous granite face sheered from the shoulder of a mountain beyond, not freestanding as it had looked from the east, but in fact a part of the mountain itself. It was as though some great cleaver in times past had severed an arm from the mountain, and this rock was the living bone of the stub.

From the cut far away to my left — and far below me now — where I had first seen the sight, a miles-long prominence of wooded slope swept upward to the west, to the very base of the huge rock which must have been several hundred feet in height to be so prominent from that distance. It stood nearly vertical, a giant's step in a higher slope which reared back toward a tall, snowcapped peak in the blue distance. At and beyond the base of the distant monolith, barely noticeable, was a break in the forest carpet where the perspective seemed a little out of plumb. A mile ahead was another promontory which might give a clearer view, so I went on.

I got my deer halfway there, cleaned and packed the meat and was coming up on high ground again when a sound stopped and chilled me. I thought I heard a voice, a man's voice, deep and rhythmic, almost chanting — a voice in which the words were lost by distance, but the tones were carried, thin and faraway. When I drew up and tried to listen, it was gone.

They played tricks with sound, these mountains. They could spook a man if he let them.

It was late afternoon when I crossed the next rise. Still intrigued by that vague discrepancy in the great stone's base, I crossed over and rode through the near arm of the forest that rose toward the rock. The stone was huge, a massive face of rock rising far into the yellowing sky above me. I rode along its base and rounded the bulk of its great south shoulder.

The small, hidden valley that opened before me there, unseen until I was just above it, was beautiful. A half-moon gap of sheltered hollow, flat-bottomed and deep in autumn graze, it spanned outward from the base of the stone to the size of a fair Missouri farmstead, outward to a protecting ring of rock ledges and steep slopes atop which was that long, aproned forest. It was a hidden park at the very heart of the great cathedral.

Except for where I now stood, or from atop the great stone — or possibly some cleft at the far end beyond my vision — the place would scarcely be noticed

38

by anyone passing through this land. There was shelter from the winds, water and wood, rich grass aplenty, and game in the hills around. It was the place I had looked for, a place to stay a while, to wait for spring. I wanted to find the Murphys but had no idea where to look, and it was time to go to ground. The only question was the Indian, and I was about half tempted to take an axe to him anyway.

Long hours passed on the ride back toward my campsite. A bright moon was high in the dark sky when I drew near and moved into the meadow to tend the black. In camp, a small, neat fire was winking back in the trees, and the Indian lay against a piece of deadfall nearby, his dark eyes glinting in the firelight.

"Take advice from a better man, white-eyes," he said without preamble. "When you're trying to be quiet, tie down your flask and pouch. I've listened to you clinking along the creek up there for an hour now."

The night air was decidedly cold, and the Indian had all the blankets around him. I pulled one off and wrapped it around my shoulders, then set out to make a meal.

His appetite had improved, if not his disposition. He ate most of the liver and several strips of haunch meat, and washed it down with coffee. After a while he said, "You may have company tomorrow." He didn't explain, just waited for me to ask why.

So I asked, "Why?"

"People near," he said. "Over on the ridge, southeast. Any Indian would have known."

With an oath I grabbed up my rifle and hurried out of the trees to look. Standing near the screening brush I let my eyes wander slowly over the faint black outline of the ridge top far beyond the sloping pasture, off to the south. For a time I saw nothing, then finally, looking away, I caught a flicker of light at the corner of my

39

eye.

It was the yellow glow of a distant campfire, almost hidden by the ridge line, far off to the southeast. I went back into the trees.

"Why didn't you tell me before?" I growled.

"Why didn't you already know?"

He wasn't going to help at all.

"All right, Henry, if you're so smart, who are they?"

Those black eyes fixed on me with malice and contempt, and a trace of evil humor. "Does it matter?" he asked evenly. "Maybe Ute or Cheyenne, maybe Arapahoc, maybe white. Makes no difference. Whoever they are, they will kill you for those horses. You are in a fix, paleface. What will you do now?"

The Murphys. It must be the Murphy brothers, looking for the expedition. The Indian was reading my mind.

"One thing I can tell you for sure. It isn't those friends you were looking for. Whoever's over there, it isn't your friends."

Being green, which I admitted to, does not necessarily mean dumb. I decided a measure of caution was in order, but I needed to know who was over there on that ridge. My fire was invisible outside the heavy grove of trees, so I let it burn but kept it small. I rolled in and slept a couple of hours, then got up, shivering in the cold night, pulled on my coat and went out onto the moonlit meadow. The horses were scattered again, far and wide across the pasture slope, but I managed to pick out the roan and round him up.

In the saddle, I checked my rifle carefully, tied down my powder flask and canteen and headed out across the meadow, angling west of south and making good time across the open country. Near the top of the ridge I entered the forest, and turned east to follow the ridge line, staying below it. It was midnight or after when I got to the knoll that marked the area where I had seen the firelight.

I left the roan there, tied a rein to a low branch, and climbed the last quarter mile on foot, using every ounce of caution I possessed and trying to make no more sound than a ghost. Atop the knoll was a cap of rock, and from there I had a fair view of the immediate area around.

The campfire was easy to see, although it had died down to coals. It was on a shelf a few hundred yards east and below where I lay, and I headed for it.

If there was a guard out I never saw him, nor he me. I came up on an outcropping just above the shelf and moved in low there to look around. There were four of them, white men, ranged around the dying fire, rolled in blankets and apparently asleep. I counted seven horses in all, picketed just beyond and below them on a patch of open grass. Various packs and utensils were strewn around in careless fashion, but I noted that each of the men had his rifle close at hand as he slept.

I was tempted for a moment to hail them and walk in, but something about them and their camp kept me where I lay. I couldn't pin it down, but they seemed out of place. By the look of their gear they were not trappers, and I could see no wagons or bundles which might indicate traders.

A slight movement brought my gaze downward to a fifth man, sitting with his back to the outcrop almost below me, bundled in blankets. He had a rifle across his lap. As I watched he filled and lit a pipe. I lay still, waiting and watching, as the cold minutes dragged by.

One of them near the fire rolled over and sat up, pulling blankets around his shoulders.

"It's damn cold," he said, and picked up a few twigs near at hand to toss on the fire. After a few moments

41

he fanned the coals with his hat until the sticks were blazing brightly, then added a few larger pieces.

"You awake, Hob?" he asked then, and the man directly below me grunted an answer.

"We goin' after them horses in the mornin' for sure?"

The man below me stretched and yawned, then relit his pipe. "Felix says so," he said.

The only horses I knew about in this part of the country were Captain Mellett's, and I strained not to miss a word.

"Don't seem exactly right," the one by the fire said. "Stock like that just grazin' out there on that slope, nobody around. Them is good horses, Hob. Somebody owns them, and that somebody ain't gonna just stand around and see them took."

"Reckon we'll see if there's anybody around come mornin'," Hobb said disinterestedly. "Ain't likely more'n two or three, or we'd have seen sign of them. Ain't likely Indians neither. They don't graze their stock open like that."

The one by the fire shook his head. "Still," he complained, "I don't fancy comin' down on them without knowin' what we're up against."

"You worry too much, Toby," the man below me said with scorn. "We'll do like we done before. Couple of us drift down there innocentlike, just passin' through, and look things over. Then if there ain't too many of them, we'll just take what we want, one way or the other."

"Just like before," the other scoffed. "Hadn't been for Felix that old man out there with them wagons would've nailed me sure. I didn't see you helpin' none, Hob Frierson."

The one called Hob bristled and his voice took on a cutting edge. "You keep harpin' on that, Toby, and you and me are goin' to have it out. Now you just shut up

42

about all that. Them people like to killed all of us, and it wasn't nobody's fault. How'd we know them kids and that old man was in that wagon holdin' guns? You ain't the only one near got killed, so just shut up about it."

The one by the fire subsided but had one final thrust to make. "And all for nothin', too. Nothin' in them wagons but junk."

An authoritative growl came from one heap of blankets on the far side of the fire. "You both better shut up and let me sleep, or I'll have your hides."

I had heard enough. Carefully, an inch at a time, I backed down off the rock, not even breathing until I got some distance away.

Night was nearly done when I got back to the creek camp and Henry was waiting, wide awake, when I came in.

"Who were they?" he asked.

To get it all straightened out in my own mind, I told him about it. He was silent for a while when I finished, then he chuckled. "Well, they're your people, white man, and it's your trouble, not mine. If it was me, I would either move those horses out of here fast or get back over there and start shootin' at first light. You might get more of them than they'd get of you."

"It's too late to move the horses," I said sourly. "And besides, you aren't me. Now shut up or I'll brain you."

He rolled over painfully and curled up tighter in the blankets.

"Damn fool," he grunted, and went back to sleep.

Chapter Five

Before full light, I moved the horses far up the meadow to the west rise, then crossed the creek, coming back toward the camp. At the high bench where the berries grew, I spurred the roan to the top and pulled up there to survey the broad valley.

It was a cold morning, pink with dawn. Frosted grass in the wide meadow showed a spiderweb pattern where I had rounded up the horses, and a broad trail to the west where I had herded them.

Squinting to sharpen the distance, I saw movement far across the way. Two horsemen were moving on the crest, starting downslope at a trot. Studying it out, I guessed they would read the sign easily and come on into the trees by the creek camp to look for whoever had moved the horses. It was time to move.

Above the camp I tied the roan in a grove and moved down toward the creek on foot. Opposite the camp I moved into a screen of brush and waited.

The Indian was gone. There was no trace of him. He was just gone. And so was the French rifle. Of all the times to have that savage gunning for my back, I thought. Well, I had my hands full right now. I would see about him later if I came through this alive.

Out on the pasture the two men had drawn up and

were looking at something on the ground. They came on. They rode easily and apparently without care or purpose, but their rifles were ready to hand across their saddles. I had both Hawkens with me, loaded and primed, and I kept one of them leveled at the riders as they moved toward the trees.

At the edge of the copse one of the riders dismounted, moved into the trees to our camp, looked around carefully and then called the other. "Get down and come in, Clay. But step light and look sharp."

In the campsite, not more than eighty feet from me, they looked around and inspected the gear I had left.

"What you make of it, Hob?" the second one asked.

"Somebody's been campin' here several days," Hob said, kneeling to study the ground around the fire. "One man, seems like, but there's somethin' almighty odd about the setup. Don't know just what."

"Smells like Injuns here," Clay said.

Hob glanced at him. "Shoot, this ain't no Indian camp, you dummy!"

"Well, if it's a white man, where is he?"

"Up the valley there with them horses be my guess," Hob said slowly. "Seen us comin' and got spooked. Tell you what, you get yourself over there behind the rocks." He pointed past my hiding place. "And I'll just sit out here pretty as you please and wait for him. If he gets the drop on me, you nail him."

There was no sense waiting any longer. I stood up and covered them with my rifle, holding the second Hawken crossways in my left hand so I could get in a fast second shot if necessary.

"Stand where you are," I told them. "Drop those guns and raise your hands."

They were cool about it all, but I suppose they decided that either I meant it or that I was scared enough I might shoot them by accident. They put their rifles on the ground and stepped back from them, raising their hands about shoulder high.

"Well, lookee here, Clay," Hob purred. "Young feller done outfoxed us sure enough. Where's your outfit, son? You ain't travelin' these mountains alone, are you?"

I didn't answer. Clay moved forward a step or so, smiled and started to lower his hands. "Look here, son, you got no call to point that thing at us," he said. "We come in friendly enough, just seein' who's around, and you act right mean about it."

I twitched the rifle barrel and he backed off again, raising his hands, the smile dissolving. There is something about looking into the muzzle of a 50-caliber Hawken that changes people's minds very quickly.

"Back up some more," I said, and they did.

"Now I don't mean you any harm," I said, "but you came here to steal horses and I can't allow that." I stepped out from the brush, crossed the creek, and walked into the campsite, not taking my eyes off them. I stood over their dropped rifles and told them, as politely as I knew how, to turn around, get their horses, and ride out.

They turned away, and as they did, the one called Clay dipped his right hand toward his belt, sidestepped and whirled, a bowie knife coming up to throw. I didn't think about it at all. I just shot him, then dropped the empty rifle and spun the spare up to cover Hob.

As I did so, I heard the click of a hammer being drawn, loud and startling in the sudden silence. I was afraid to look around, but I saw Hob's eyes light up as he looked past me. There was the sound of a shot, and I jumped like a cat. But nothing hit me. I heard a thump and the rattling of stones on the creek bank behind me, and saw Hob's expression change again, to amazement and then to anger.

Henry's taunting voice came from behind me somewhere. "You ought to watch your backside closer, white-

46

eyes. This one had you dead to rights."

I held off the feeling of relief that threatened to relax me, promising I would enjoy it at leisure sometime later. Gesturing toward the base of a tree nearby I told Hob to sit down there, and he did as he was told. With a pack strap I secured his wrists so that his arms were drawn back around the tree. Only then did I look around.

A man lay dead on the far bank of the creek, facedown, almost in the water, a rifle beside him. He was the one I had seen by the outlaws' campfire, the one called Toby.

Clay was still alive, but my shot had shattered his right shoulder. The big knife he had tried to throw lay on the ground near him.

Henry was up in the rocks across the creek. I got Hob and Clay secured, piled their weapons out of the way and crossed the creek. When I helped Henry down out of the rocks his face was paler than mine. I reloaded the French rifle and handed it back to him without a word, then picked up all the other guns around and tied them in a bundle, all but my Hawken.

"Henry," I said. "I'd appreciate it if you'd keep these two quiet here. I'm going to be gone a while."

He looked at me speculatively but said nothing.

At the sight of the Indian, Hob's face took on an ugly cast. "I thought you was alone." He spat. "Didn't know you had a heathen friend."

Henry answered him mildly enough, but with a wicked edge to his voice. "I am no friend of his, mister. I just like to kill white men."

There were five rifles in the bundle I had tied, Billy's Hawken, the three outlaws' guns, and Henry's old musket. They were all loaded. With these and my rifle, I headed back across the creek toward where I had left the roan.

Henry called after me, "Are you going to say thanks?"

"No," I told him, and went on up the hill.

I took the long way around, but pushed the roan and made good time of it. In a little over an hour I was at the foot of the ridge knoll where I had been in the dark hours of that morning, and quietly carried the six rifles up to the top, then crawled with them to the outcrop overlooking the outlaw camp. The remaining two were there, as I had hoped, putting a midday meal on the fire.

One was a big brute of a man, heavy through the shoulders and with a full black beard. He looked like a bear. The other was a slim, whipcord man with nervous hands and a deep scar down one side of his face.

In the distance beyond the camp, their pack animals were picketed close together, packs strapped atop them, ready for departure. Their saddle horses were nearer, rein-tied at a stand of young willows. It looked as though they were ready to move out.

I lifted Billy's Hawken and as the slim man picked up a pot from the fire, I put a ball through it. The sound of the rifle and the explosion of the pot had a better effect than I could have hoped for. The big man let out a rolling curse and heaved backward, away from the fire, missing as he grabbed for his rifle, and then tumbling off the little rock ledge where he had been sitting. The slim man shouted and turned just as I brought up another rifle and splattered a ball on a rock at the noses of the pack horses. The animals reared, tore loose their picket lines, and scattered, running. The next rifle was up, and I hurried a shot toward the big man as he tried to get to his feet. He fell again, then scuttled into the cover of some rocks at the east end of the campsite. The slim man was on his feet, his mouth open, and I aimed the next shot at an ornate powder horn hanging from his belt. It exploded against his leg and he fell, then rolled under some brush.

The next gun I grabbed was Henry's musket, and its boom resounded through the crags around us as the huge ball kicked up gravel at the feet of the outlaws' saddle mounts. A moment later these horses were following the pack animals in a dash across the countryside.

Both the men were out of sight now. I raked the empty guns together, slipped the sling around them, and carrying these and my still-loaded Hawken, I slid and sprinted down the backside of the knoll, mounted the roan, and wheeled him back the way I had come. One of the outlaws' pack horses had stampeded over this way and was running down the meadow slope ahead of me. As I overtook him, I grabbed his lead and headed on at a dead run, straight down across the meadow toward my own camp.

I was well out on the grass when I heard a shot from the top of the ridge, and I turned in the saddle and answered it with my Hawken, then ducked low on the roan's neck and headed home.

It would take them a while to round up their horses, and it might take them a while longer to sort out their wits. I hoped so. I wanted to be a long way gone before they got organized again.

In the camp Henry was sitting up, the rifle across his lap, a bowie knife in his hand, and a smirk on his face. The renegade, Hob, still tied to the tree where I had left him, looked scared to death, and I wondered for a moment what they might have been talking about.

I stripped the saddle from the lathered roan and put it on Billy's black, which I had herded from the tall grass as I came in. Then I reloaded all the rifles, went out and got three of our pack horses and Henry's spotted mustang pony, and saddled and packed these.

"Let's go, Henry," I said, and helped him onto his horse. He still had the French rifle and I told him, belatedly, "If you plan to shoot me with that, do it later. Right now we've got to travel."

We left nothing at the creekside camp except three outlaws. One was dead, one wounded, and one tied to a tree.

We lit out upstream, following the rocky creek bank, moving as fast as the horses would drive.

The Indian looked as though he would die right there on that mustang's back, but he held on, and we moved on.

My fortune was increasing steadily. I now had sixteen horses and one armed hostile. This morning I had only thirteen horses and a busted Indian.

Upstream about three miles I pointed the herd to the right, up the cut bank, and we scrambled over sliding rock and shale banks to the top of the ridge. We ran west a mile or more, over table rock and gravel. The horses settled to an easy run, and I knew they were good for a few miles, so I just nudged the black and kept pace.

We were miles back into the mountains before I called a halt. From the ridge top we had angled to the north again, down a rocky shoulder, and into a winding canyon which turned back to the east. Leaving the canyon, we had backtracked a mile and then cut south to another rock ridge and followed it.

I pulled up at a pool of spring water in the back of a deep, secluded canyon, helped Henry down off the paint, unsaddled and unpacked the horses, and made camp. The horses were lathered from the run but still in fair shape. I rubbed them all down and turned them out on the grass floor of the canyon to graze. When the fire was going, I put a pot of coffee on and gave Henry the first cup, using utensils from the well-stocked supply pack on the animal I had gained from the outlaws.

From where we were now, I judged, it was an easy drive to the standing rock. It was there I intended to go.

Chapter Six

For a week or more the weather had been clear and fine, but now it changed. A rising wind whipped the shrubbery above us on the canyon wall, and chill gathered around us in the bottom. It grew dark quickly, with heavy clouds marching through the peaks to the west and the north so that as the sun went down, its rays died, swallowed by the mountains.

I had started a fire near the spring, but soon moved it back under a rock ledge and added more fuel. I half carried Henry into the curve of the sheltered place and bedded him down there, with the fire before him and the reflecting rock behind. The wound in his back had opened again. He had lost some blood, but it was not as bad as it might have been.

"Do you know how to sew buckskins?" he asked as I cleaned the wound and rebandaged it.

"No, I don't."

"I do. Save those deer hides and any others you come across. Winter will come early this year." He paused, then asked. "Do you know where you're going?"

"Yes, I found a place."

"Those are bad whites back there. They may follow."

"Yes."

"What did you do over there today?"

51

I told him about it, briefly, and for just a moment his habitual cynicism faded into a spark of admiration.

"You counted coup," he said. "If you tried, white-eyes, maybe you could think like an Indian."

It rained during the night, a cold, freezing rain, and I went out and gathered the horses back under a lip of rock near our shallow cave. The animals crowded in, keeping warm.

Overhead the wind was howling, and the brush whipped as driving rain pounded into the canyon. Brilliant lightning outlined the walls in stark relief, and thunder sounding like cannon fire, rolled through the mountains.

I was cold and wet, dead tired, frightened, and sore. But after a meal, and as the fire started warming the stone behind us, I rolled into a blanket and slept, relaxed and lulled by the sounds of a mountain storm.

Except once.

It happened deep into the night. The rain had subsided but distant thunder still rolled. I came awake with a sound in my ears that I couldn't quite remember. Then I heard it again. Between echoes of thunder, while lightning shadows danced abruptly on the canyon's serrated walls, I heard a voice. Far off, tiny among the elements, but still distinct, a man's voice was raised in counterpoint:

"And the Lord said unto Moses, go, get thee down;

"For thy people, which thou brought out of the land of Egypt, have corrupted themselves.

"They have turned aside by the Way which I commanded them;

"They have made a molten calf . . ."

It faded as renewed lightning sundered the sky and thunder rolled in with the sound of an apocalypse. I saw Henry up on his hands, his eyes straining outward into the storm, his face haunted.

"Death wind," he said. "The ghost who walks . . ."

The rest was in Ute or Pawnee. It was the first time I

52

had seen him frightened. He was still mumbling when I went back to sleep.

The storm ended before morning, but the sky was low and dark as we breakfasted and packed to move on. Tendrils of cloud clung low on the mountain peaks, blotting out all but the lowest portions, and it was cold.

Henry was pale and silent, and remained so as we started the herd back down the canyon and then out across a rocky flat, heading south.

The circuitous route we had followed had taken us far off the path I had used before in coming to the altar-stone rock, but by cutting back south we came late in the day to a ravine I recognized and soon were on top of the crest from which I had studied the great natural cathedral. Clouds obscured its face, and it was less impressive than when I had viewed it before. But it was still enough to arouse a superstitious awe in the Indian. We went on, and finally herded the horses down the precipitous cut into the hidden valley at the foot of the altar. It was everything I had hoped for and more.

The floor of the cut was maybe a hundred acres in size, flat and heavy with grass and wild oats. Back near the vertical wall, which was a projection of the base of the monument stone, was a deep basin of clear water fed by some spring under the rock itself. The water fed from the basin into two lesser pools. At one place, about midway along the outer ring of the valley, the ridge wall surrounding it was lower for a space and heavily wooded with pine. And off at one side, back from the rock, was a sandstone face heavily undercut by ancient waters. A good place for shelter for both men and horses—and for Indians, since I had about given up on Han-Ra-Hay's dying right away. Deer and elk signs here and there indicated the chance to lay in a supply of meat before the winter snows.

Chapter Seven

For a while I worked harder than I had ever worked before. There was a shelter and corral to be built for the horses, and I set to with axe and tow lines to bring in a supply of long, slender pine logs, snaking them down from the ridge. With the axe and some rope, I built a rough stone boat and hauled stone down from a fall back of the basin. Mounds of stone served as corners to anchor the corral poles, and walls of stone and a pole and sod roof formed a barn of sorts in which the animals could shelter. I trenched water from the basin into the corral.

A little to one side, and backing on the sandstone ledge, I piled stone into walls about three feet high and laid logs atop that for another three feet. Then I roofed the whole thing over with a high-peaked ridgepole and sod roof snug enough to get by.

At the end of a couple of weeks I set off on the roan, with pack horses, to find meat. It was plentiful. In two days I was back with the dressed carcasses of a bull elk and a buffalo calf, and a pack full of wild berries and roots.

Building a pit fire and pole rack a short distance from the cabin, I started jerking most of the meat, while the Indian took the hides to stretch and cure. He was getting around some, still sore but moving. A couple of days later

I went out again and brought in two deer, then started the whole process all over again.

After the rain, it had remained overcast and chill for several days, then a northwind cleared the air and left the weather brilliant and biting cold, warming some during the day but crisping again each night. Several mornings I cracked ice on the trench for the horses to drink. The animals were sleek and fat, and their coats were growing shaggy with winter fur. Little by little the air turned warmer in the daytime, although the nights remained chill, until finally there was a spell of days almost like high-country summer.

I had been thinking of scouting the top of the standing rock. So on a clear morning I saddled the black and headed down the pasture to the back canyon. There a narrow, rock-strewn trail led back away from the great stone, winding through a crack that would be impassable when snow fell. I had made a habit of using only this trail out of the valley.

From the top of the gorge, emerging into the wide pine woods, I reined to the right and nudged the black up the slope. We made good time for about a half mile. Then the route grew steeper, and I angled off to the right, taking the slope at a diagonal, climbing upward and east.

The rising sun slanted in through the pine, quartering on my face, and the whole world was generally a pleasant place to be. Cresting out on a slope, I rounded the hump of it and entered a stand of brilliant aspen, rustling in the morning sun, white trunks so thick in places that I had to go around entire groves to get past. Here and there among them were the blackened stumps of long-dead pines, and scattered around in the open spots were young pines seeking the sun.

From a knoll thrusting above the aspen woods I could see mile on mile of mountain wilderness, the higher peaks to the west now brilliant with snow, the somber forests below me carpeting a land of slopes and valleys, mountainsides and canyons. A short way further the world sheered away into nothing, dropping from sight into misted void. Beyond, far away, the carpet of pines spread tiny in the distance toward a realm of crags and rough terrain — long canyons stretching away to the east flanked by finger ridges and wide, deep valleys.

Turning, I rode through the last of the aspens, between thickets of spruce, and came out atop the great stone altar. The view was awesome. I tied the black and walked to the edge.

Below, hundreds of feet straight down, was the hidden valley. Several of the horses were in view, grazing on the open meadow. A thin wisp of smoke lifted from the cabin, hung silver in the morning light, then dissipated on a stray breeze around the face of the granite cliff.

Beyond the valley was the broad stretch of forest, furred and dark green, spreading back toward the breaks where the canyons began. Far to the east, a glint of water in a canyon caught my eye and I followed the line of it off into the misty miles. Out there was the meadow where Billy was buried.

Off to the right, far but discernible, was the canyon where Captain Mellett's expedition had died.

To the north was ragged country, and I was gazing out there, intrigued by the vastness of it, when I saw smoke. It was just a wisp, a wraith, on the crest of a distant ridge.

Probably Indians. I had begun to doubt now that those renegades had tried to follow us, and anyway that smoke was far off the route we had taken. Lost, possibly, but I didn't think so. It might, however, be a good idea to have a look up that way while the weather held.

I squatted at the edge of that tall cliff and concentrated on the distance, idly fingering the cool, soft earth beside me. Then I noticed it. I had found it with my fingers, but not with my mind, until now. A crisp impression in the dirt between bits of rock — a boot track.

It was a jolt. But now that I looked, it was there, sharp and clear in the soft earth caught at the altar's crown. Not a moccasin. A boot.

It was smaller than mine, and studded in the sole in the usual fashion of mulehide boots. Small, but not smaller than the average man's print: My own boots were larger than normal, as was my general proportion these past couple of years.

Someone had stood here, a white man, on top of the altar stone. And recently.

Taking my time, I scouted back away from the precipice and found part of another track in a bit of soft ground among the rock, but not enough to make out a trail. It was spooky. I felt that I was being watched, although I was certain it was just imagination. Nevertheless I wasted no time getting back to my horse and heading down the mountainside, back the way I had come.

I found nothing more out of the ordinary. Whoever had stood atop that rock was gone now and had not returned that I could see.

The Indian and I had conversed little since we entered the valley, each of us being busy, I with building and he with mending. As I prowled around the valley later, he was watching me, and in the evening I caught him regarding me with that knowing smirk on his copper face.

"What are you looking at?" I glared back at him, irritated.

"A nervous white man," he answered after a moment. "Spirits are in this place. You feel them, too."

"No spirit makes boot tracks that I ever heard of," I snapped, then settled back and told him what I had seen. The coal-black eyes remained inscrutable as I talked. His face was impassive.

But when I spoke of the smoke in the distance he spat out, "You think Indians would be so careless? If you saw it, it was white man's smoke."

A thought struck me then. "Henry, you said once my two friends weren't coming back. How did you know?"

He grinned. "Uinay and me, we found your marker up there in that ring wall. That was after you had gone with the horses. We changed it to point another way."

There were times now and again when I regretted not having brained that Pawnee back when the mood was on me. This was one of those times. "And which way," I asked, "did you point it?"

"As I recall, it was due west."

Due west of there would be north of here. North, where I had seen the smoke.

The following morning there was frost on the meadow and a skim of ice again on the basin. I breakfasted and saddled the roan, and slung a light pack on one of the other animals. With one Hawken slung from the saddle-bow and the other in hand I headed out across the valley, up into the pine woods and turned north. Somewhere out in those hills, if they were still alive, were the Murphy brothers. I intended to find them.

To get my bearings I circled around on a line with the great stone landmark and skirted the foot of the rise which climbed toward its distant top. One thing I found right there—the paw marks of a big old bear with a crippled foot. Up on the mountainside yesterday I had seen a scratching tree where a big bear had left its mark, torn bark well above my head. I wasn't the only one who had claimed this territory.

Chapter Eight

William and Tad Murphy were New Yorkers, two of about a dozen children of a couple that farmed and kept a greengrocery in Queensborough. Near of an age, they packed their satchels when times got hard and went west, leaving two less mouths to feed at home. They worked for a time on a canal gang pushing toward the Ohio, put in and lost a crop down in Missouri, and were signed as deck hands on a river boat when they decided to throw in with the captain at Independence. They were decent men, and I certainly needed them now.

It was near evening when I came to the general area where I had seen that smoke, and a long, hard day of riding was behind the roan and me. In straight distance, it would have been no more than a dozen miles, but there are no straight distances in the front range of the Shining Mountains. For a landmark I had picked out a prominent broken peak that thrust above the timberline like a lone sentinel in those miles of crumpled landscape, and kept pointed toward it through the day. And I used a trick I had learned from Will Farris.

"A travelin' man in bad country does well to look on his backtrail," he once said. And he was talking about more than unfriendly folk. It isn't hard to go someplace when you have a landmark in front of you. But things look different from the backside, and it pays to stop now and then and see where you have been. That way you store up new landmarks to use when you try to go back.

It was well I did that. When I came to the place I judged the smoke to have been and looked back over those miles from the top of a spur standing over that ridge, I couldn't make out the cathedral rock at all, though I knew just where it was. From where I was standing it was just another feature in the faroff landscape.

I scouted around for an hour or more, with the sun going down through some strung-out clouds behind the great peaks, and had about decided I'd have to wait for morning when I found the cold camp. There wasn't much to see. Back in the shelter of a cedar grove there had been a fire, and the ground had been swept for bedding. In last light, I made out a few horse droppings in the bleaching grass just below, and a few features of the campsite that told me Henry was right. This was no Indian camp. If it had been, chances are I never would have found it in the first place. There had been three or four people here and some horses. I couldn't tell where they had gone.

There was nothing more to do until morning, so I moved off a ways, found a sheltered spot and made camp for the night. In the morning there would be tracks to follow.

I made early breakfast by first light and then set out to check the tracks I had spotted the night before. They were clear enough, and I made good time.

The land there swelled steadily upward toward the west, and the high peaks beyond looked so close in the morning air you could have stuck out your arm and touched them. Snow was well down on their flanks, and the wind coming off them was cold.

About midday, high on a slope where the timber was thin and the going was rough, I stopped to rest the roan in some stunted grass, and hunkered down behind a boulder to eat, out of the wind. The occasional tracks I had been following were still pointing west, angling up the shoulder of the mountain I had been on since mid-morning.

Comfort, a simple matter of being in the sun and out of the wind, got the best of me, and I dozed there for a while. The voice that woke me nearly scared me to death.

"Just sit still, mister. Don't move a muscle 'til I get a look at you."

My head came up so hard I banged it on the rock behind me, and there, standing a few feet away, was Tad Murphy, rifle at his shoulder and its bore dead on me. When I looked up he stared, and then a big grin split his sunburned face.

"Randy, as I live and breathe," he whooped. "Randall Kerry, wherever have you been?"

It was a little hard to return that happy grin right then, because he was still pointing that rifle at me, hammer back and finger white across the trigger, and I swear he had forgotten it was there.

I brought both hands up. "Tad, it sure would be a shame if you killed me right now."

He blushed redder than he already was and lowered the gun, letting the hammer off cock. A moment later we were wringing each other's hands, beating each other on the back and both trying to talk at the same time. Bits and pieces of what he said were, ". . . Found your marker . . . followin' along . . . beginnin' to wonder . . . lost sure as the everlastin' . . . need to talk to the captain. . . ."

The last brought me up short, and I held him out at

arm's length. "Tad, they're gone. I'm all that's left. That is, me and you and William, now. Where is he? There's so much to tell."

I was still spitting out words too fast to make sense, but I saw it start to soak in and stopped. He kept on grinning, but the grin just hung there while he tried to take in what I had said. He was all set to laugh at the joke, and then figured out it wasn't one.

"He isn't with me," he said directly. "I couldn't find him, but we can find him when I catch up with . . . catch up with . . ." He stuck there, and the words he was looking for weren't available.

We would have to get it all sorted out, but first things first. "If it isn't William, then who's with you, Tad? I found sign —"

"Oh, yeah, I got some people. They're up ahead. But why, Randy? What happened? What do you mean, they're gone? Where's the captain, and the Pastor and Rollo? Ain't you come to fetch us?"

We weren't getting anywhere at all. I picked up my rifle and gear and said, "Come on, Tad. I'll tell you all about it, but let's go see who you got."

They were in a break just off the dim trail I had been following: an old man, a girl, and a little boy, and both man and boy had rifles on us as we came in through the scrub. When they saw Tad, they lowered them and stood waiting. All except the girl. I swear she looked at me like I'd come early to a social and ate all the frosting off the cake.

It wasn't just for me, though. She looked at Tad the same way, and I had the impression that look was standard fixture. She looked like she was mad enough to spit nails and planned to stay that way.

The man's name was Raymond Sneed. He was grandfather to the young ones, Becky and Jesse Frost, their mother's father. Becky was a pretty little thing, for certain, about sixteen and slight, with a lot of blond hair peeking from under an old slouch hat that shaded the face of an irritated angel. I couldn't quite make her out, and she didn't say enough to help any. Her brother was a determined-looking ten-year-old with the same sunshine hair and blue eyes, which had lit on the scalp at my belt and kept getting bigger as he speculated on what it was.

I howdido'd them while Tad pointed around and named names, and all the time I was noticing they had a coffee pot sitting beside campfire coals. I allowed a cup would go real well right now and glanced at the girl, Becky, who was nearest the fire. But Tad jumped in and said, "Yessir, I bet it would," and tended to the pouring.

As he handed it to me he warned, quietly, "You don't want to mess with that girl, Randy. Somethin' sure enough wrong with her."

We spent the better part of the afternoon there. I told them what had happened, about the expedition and the massacre, and it wasn't a happy time at all. Several times as I talked Tad Murphy turned away. I had had some time to get used to it. He hadn't.

When I described the run-in with those white renegades, they all listened sharp, and Mr. Sneed said, "It was them. Briole and them."

"You know them, do you?"

"I know them, and I guess you do, too. It was them killed these children's papa, and I'll swear I know them. It was Felix Briole's bunch."

The second time he said the name it hit home.

Felix Briole. Anybody who's read a newspaper or listened to the talk around a general store, anybody who's been in Missouri or the rivers country, knew about Felix Briole. Just plain crazy mean, that's what they said about him. He had killed some men out in

Missouri, and done some robbing and bushwhacking, and as he went along he put together a band that had roamed up and down the Kansas borders for a couple of years. Everybody knew about them, and nobody ever seemed to stop them.

Then about a year or so back they had ridden into a little town, killed a lot of people and burned several buildings to the ground. The story had it they had hung two men right out there in the street, just for the fun of it, and made their families stand and watch. Two of the people killed in that town were women, and one was a little child. The Briole bunch had dropped out of sight a year ago.

As I thought about it, names slipped into place, and faces came along from back on that mountain creek to match them. The one called Hob. That would be Hob Frierson, who they said was a fugitive from back East somewhere. And there was a Clay Shandy, a Missourian. The one I had shot through the shoulder, the one with the knife, had been Clay. One of the bunch was Mercer Cate, a Canadian renegade whose reputation was made long before he hooked up with Briole. I pictured the slim nervous man with the scar on his face, whose powder flask I had hit. There were a couple of others whose names I couldn't call. And Felix Briole was their leader.

It hit me right where I lived. Those men back there had scared me proper. But knowing who they were now, that scared me even worse.

"You shoulda' done 'em all in, Randy," Tad was saying, seriously.

"I should have got hell — beg pardon, miss — out of there right off, Tad. That's what I should have done."

The boy was sitting there, fingering that long Kentucky rifle which seemed never to leave his small hands. Now he looked at me with moist eyes. "Those men back there," he said, "they killed our Pa."

They had set out in mid-summer with a wagon train bound for California, these three and the children's father, a widower whose name was Reuben Frost. For some reason that I never caught, Frost had decided to leave the train along the way and strike out on his own path. For two weeks they had inched their old wagon across the hills and breaks west of the high plains. And then, with the mountains just ahead, they broke an axle for which there was no spare.

Briole's gang had come up on them there. What happened was confused, but the outlaws had killed Frost and been driven off by the others firing from within the wagon bed. Either driven off or, more likely, saw nothing worth the taking.

That girl now, with that old hat and hidden in a wagon bed, would not have seemed a girl. What had the outlaw said when I listened at their camp? An old man and some kids?

With three horses left and what they could carry, the three had headed for the nearest shelter—those mountains just a few miles off.

"I come on them while I was looking for William," Tad said. "We heard something down aways from the pasture, and he rode out to see what it was. When he didn't come back I went to look. Found where his tracks met some others, but I lost them in a little ways. So I circled around, to see if I could tell where that other bunch came from, saw some smoke off a ways and went to look. I figured I'd bring 'em to the captain," he added lamely. "He'd know what to do."

He brought them back to the walled meadow, found the herd gone and a stone marker pointing westward, and followed it.

"I don't know where William is, either," I told him. "But I found a hole to hide in for a while."

That evening we got down off the cold shoulder of that mountain, then pointed south toward my landmarks and made camp. And those people were tuckered. The old man, Sneed, was a wiry old fellow and seemed in better condition than anyone, but we were all ready for a night's rest.

Sneed rode a reformed draft horse that had been part of their wagon team. The girl and boy rode double on a buckskin. They had another horse packed with boxes and bales salvaged from their wagon.

All along, I'd had the feeling Mr. Sneed was looking me over pretty carefully. Just before full dark he drew Tad and me aside for some words.

"We're beholden to you fellows," he said. "The children and me, we'd have perished soon if you hadn't come upon us, Mr. Murphy."

"That's all right." Tad shuffled his feet. "I was lost, too."

"But nonetheless," Sneed pushed on, "we're beholden. And I reckon we're bound to you now until we can get someplace where we can see to ourselves." He paused and gave us each a level stare, first Tad and then me.

"We're bound to you," he repeated, "and I make you both to be decent young men. There's a thing I'd ask of you now."

We just waited.

"I would like your word on a matter," he continued. "I've been around a time, myself, and I know how some things are. It's about my granddaughter."

I looked at Tad, and he looked at me, puzzled.

"She's of an age now," the old man went on, determinedly, "and you'll both have noticed she's a right pretty little thing. I'd have your word, sirs, that you'll take no advantage . . ."

Tad sputtered, "No offense, sir, but a man would be

crazy to try getting close to that one. She is a hellion."

Mr. Sneed nodded. "No offense taken. I admit, right now, that is the case. But I expect it will pass, you see. Too much has happened to Becky in too little time. The girl you see there ain't Becky, rightly."

I looked over by the fire. The girl I saw there, scowling into the fire, still looked like bad weather fixing to happen.

"You can set your mind at ease, Mr. Sneed," I said. "I won't bother your girl, and you have my word on it."

Tad was thoughtful. "I reckon I follow you, sir. I've had sisters, and they are almighty changeable. But if it eases your mind you have my bond as well."

Sneed gave us both another long look and then nodded.

"That satisfies me," he said.

I couldn't help wondering what a Becky free of whatever burden this one bore would be like. But I meant what I'd said. I wouldn't have thought any more about trying to cozy up to that girl than a man would think about sticking his hand into a fire.

We didn't talk much more that night. All of us were occupied with our own thoughts.

It took us more of the next day, starting early, to get to a point where I could see Cathedral Rock, and most of the day after that to get there. I had put my saddle on Mr. Sneed's draft horse for his comfort, and I was riding bareback.

I don't recall to this day whether I had told them about Henry. And I surely didn't think of what might happen when we came around the sandstone shoulder by my hard-built horse corral. But it happened.

Henry was standing there by the corral when we came up. In his buckskins, high moccasins, and beads, with that long black hair braided and tied, he was about as savage a sight as you would want to see. The boy, Jesse, saw him at the same time I did and instantly the long rifle came up and the hammer went back. Before any of us could more than blink, the rifle roared and a shower of splinters exploded from the corral post. Henry dived full-length for the shelter of a cairn of stones, and the buckskin horse reared and threw both its young passengers off over its rump.

In a moment before reaction set in, Tad whistled long and low and breathed, "Well, I be damn."

The Indian's head came up over the pile of rock and his French rifle came level. I swung the Hawken and thumbed back the hammer and Tad's rifle came around to cover him. "Henry," I roared, "put that away or I'll shoot you."

He hesitated, and Tad sighted in on him. Finally he stood up, slowly, lowering the rifle at his side. "That damned kid tried to kill me," he barked, and his eyes blazed cold fire in the fading light.

Sneed gasped beside me. "By the great heaven, that Indian talks white."

I turned to the children who had been pitched head over heels onto the turf.

The girl was just picking herself up, her eyes huge and angry. "Darn you, Jesse! If you had to do that you could at least hit him!"

The boy was busily tamping a load into the Kentucky. I reached and grabbed it from his hands. He glared at me, then hauled off and whacked my horse on the rump, open handed, with all his strength.

An unsaddled horse is slick on top. The roan just disappeared from under me, and I hit the' ground hard.

I learned something else about Indians right then. When something strikes them funny, they laugh just like civilized people. At any rate, by the time I picked myself up and favored that boy with a glare I hoped would wither his skinny bones, the tension of the moment was past. Sneed and the Indian from then on had the air between them of friends who had enjoyed a situation together. The boy didn't crack a smile, but neither did he try to kill Henry again. And that girl, while she didn't say anything, turned those angry eyes on me as I brushed off my dignity, and for a moment they didn't look quite so angry. There was a peculiar look in her eye right then, like she might decide to smile, and if she did it would be something to see. But she didn't.

I helped Tad unpack the animals and turned them into the corral, and Henry got a cooking fire going.

Chapter Nine

I had pretty well made up my mind to sit the winter out right here and maybe try to make it out with the horses in the spring. And for a fact, there wasn't anywhere to go that seemed likely. We were pretty well hemmed in here, with high passes to the west and south, and those great desolate plains to the east. In the spring we might make it.

So keeping an eye on the weather, I worked like a mule for the next several days. I rightened up the cabin, enlarged the corral, and brought in all the hay I could cut. The old man and Jesse pitched right in and helped, and even that Indian did such work as he could with his wound still mending.

Tad stayed gone a lot. In the morning he would saddle up early and ride out, first this way and then another, sometimes gone more than a day. He was fidgeting about his brother and just couldn't stay put long.

He was careful about trails, though, leaving none to follow back to this place. And each time he came back he would tell me what he had found and what he had seen. With all the traps we had, I talked some of pelting. We might pick up a nice stake through the winter, both of us working at it. He found a place he named "three peaks" about twenty miles west where there was a deep mountain lake with streams running into it and plenty of beaver dams and muskrat digs. Between us we knew a bit about trapping, and we shared what we knew. And come spring, maybe we could head for Sante Fe. It was something to lean on, at any rate.

But then he'd be gone again, tailing the country over for sign of his brother.

A time or two when I could break loose, I rode back up to the top of the great rock, still bothered by that footprint up there. I found bear mark again — he was a big one sure enough — but no more sign of the man who left the boot print. Each time I went up there, though, I took food. And when I went back it would be gone. I decided I must be feeding that bear.

The girl, Becky, was a puzzle. Being around her was like a long spell of bad weather. When we had brought them to the cabin, the first thing she had done was march in and throw out Henry's and my bedding. Then she moved herself and Jesse and Mr. Sneed in. From that point Tad and I and the Indian made do outside with a blanket strung from the corral bars to break the wind. She rarely spoke, and when she did, I always wished she hadn't.

Like, "Don't you dare come in that door. This place is already a pigsty without you tracking in. Back home we at least had a floor." And, "Back home we had proper windows. If I couldn't build a house better than this I wouldn't even try."

It was usually "back home" this and "back home" that. Once I tried to tell her that it wasn't my fault she wasn't back home right now, and I wished to heaven she were. She stamped her foot at that and lit into me all over again about blaming her father. I noticed when she was out about the cabin she was careful never to look around her at the mountains. It was

71

though she just didn't want to admit they were there.

I was beginning to feel like maybe it was my fault she was stranded out here in this godforsaken wilderness. But she treated Tad the same way, and I knew it wasn't his fault, either.

One time, while I was working on the cabin door, Henry wandered in from someplace and went inside to stash some hides. He came right back out again, with the hides sailing after him. He picked them up and went someplace else, cussing in about three languages. On the way he turned back once and scowled at the cabin. "Squaw," he said.

Mr. Sneed was helping me put up hay when he stopped for a minute and said, "Son, I hope you don't take too unkindly to little Becky. She's awful unhappy."

I could see that, but it still wasn't my fault.

On top of that, one day she caught up the three of us, Tad and me and the Indian, and put us all in the corral with Jesse and that long gun of his, watching us while she went off to the little pond beyond the cabin to bathe. I believe she thought all three of us were savages. Of course, one of us was for a fact. But she had no reason to treat us all that way. And when she came back, fussing and fuming, I had the feeling that she even blamed us all for the water in the mountain pond being cold.

At any rate it went on like that, the days passing and the snow moving farther down the peaks to the west and south of us. And early on a chill morning Tad Murphy was up and sniffing the air.

"Randy, I got to go," he said, looking off to the south. "I got to find William, and he's nowhere around here."

"The snow's coming," I told him. He shuffled his feet a bit and shook his head.

"That's what I'm thinking," he said. "It's been too

long now. If he was around, I would have found him—one way or another."

He hemmed around a little. Then he said, "I got to go south. That's where William went."

"Those passes are closing up, Tad," I told him, though he could see that for himself.

"I know, but I can still get through. Randy, I'm going to Santa Fe. William's got to be there."

Dawn was breaking, chill and overcast, when he headed out down the valley. He had his saddle horse, and one of those I got from Felix Briole's bunch with a pack on it. At the foot of the rise, before he entered the climbing gorge, he turned and lifted a hand to us.

A whining wind was wandering through the peaks, but later in the day it died down and the clouds moved lower. By mid-afternoon the first flakes of snow were falling. The horses out in the pasture moved in and bunched under the shelter roof in the open corral, and I cracked the ice in the trough for them, pitched some hay up by the back wall, picked up the bedding that was out, and headed into the cabin.

It was warm inside, and my fingers and toes ached for a while until the heat settled in and the blood got to circulating. I tossed the bedding against the back wall and said to the place in general, "We'll make room in here." Mr. Sneed and the children were already indoors, and Henry came in a few minutes later, numb with cold.

Somewhere out there, heading south, was Tad Murphy, and some of us at least wished him well.

We sat on robes and blankets around a pit fire, chewing on jerky and drinking coffee. There is nothing to compare with a warm fire and snug walls when the snow is falling outside.

Henry was cleaning the French rifle, and I got down the Hawkens and started cleaning them. Jesse watched us for a while, then he pulled the load from his long gun and swabbed it out. Mr. Sneed lit up a pipe and sat staring into the fire, his thoughts deep and far away.

Becky busied herself putting on another pot of coffee, and I noticed how the firelight caught her hair when she turned, and how there were shadows deep in her eyes. For a time at least she had nothing to say, though her actions as she worked still managed to convey a great and general anger. She never smiled, that one, but I thought it would be a wondrous sight if she did.

Henry was watching the boy clean the long rifle. "You need practice with that," he said, and Jesse flashed him a sharp look.

"I almost got you with it, didn't I?"

"Almost counts for nothing," the Indian said, pleasantly enough. "What if I'd been a bear?"

"You ain't no bear," Jesse pointed out, his young voice strong and angry. "You ain't nothin' but a thievin' redskin."

Henry considered it. "That," he admitted, "is a fact. But I'm talking about your shooting." He looked around. "See that chink in the wall there, boy? All right, you stand up now and let's see how you lay that rifle on it."

Jesse did as he was told, and Henry shook his head sadly.

"You would miss it by a foot," he said. "Try getting your head right down there on the stock. That's it, bend your neck. Put your cheekbone right in behind your thumb there. That's better—now how come you're doing that?"

"Doing what?" Jesse sounded exasperated.

"Shutting your left eye that way. You shooting at the whole chink or just half of it?"

"I have to do that to see through the sight," the boy complained.

"No you don't." Henry got up, stood behind him and placed him with his face into the stock. "Now open both eyes, boy," he instructed. "Look down the sights with one of them, and let the other one figure the range for you. Now don't tighten up. Shooting a rifle's just like pointing your finger. Except it's a lot more final."

When he sat back down by the fire I asked him, "Where did you learn all that?"

"Hanging around the army post at Westport," he said. "Us thievin' redskins spend a lot of time hanging around army posts. Learn a lot that way."

When I drew the hide back from the little front window and looked out, the world was dark grey and filled with falling snow. It was picking up, blanketing everything with a mantle of winter white, bringing a hush to the mountains. I pulled on my coat, reloaded my Hawken, and walked outside.

I could see no farther than fifty yards in any direction. All around was just the shadowed pattern of sifting, falling snow. The ground was already covered by an inch or more and soon would be deep in white fluff. I checked on the horses, and they were doing fine, huddled cozily into the sheltered part of the corral, their shaggy coats dark and dry. Even during those few minutes the snowfall had become heavier, and the light was fading. It was a wonderful, peaceful, hushed world with bits of icy down clinging and coating everything at hand.

When I returned to the cabin I was white with snow. Taking a last look around, I knew that we were all going to stay pretty close to the fire for the next few days.

And stepping through the cabin door from that

clean, icy mountain air I knew something else. Some of us were going to need a bath. And no better time than the present, while the ponds were still open.

With my mind made up, I dug around until I found some yellow soap and a bundle of muslin scraps. Then I hung up my hat and coat, stripped down to my flannels, took the soap in one hand and a rifle in the other, and strode out the door as a gasp sounded behind me.

I danced for the lower pond, a few yards down from the cabin. I waded in to my knees then plunged in full length, gasping for breath and listening to the rime ice crackle around the edges. Thoroughly wet, I scrubbed quickly with the soap, went under again, then grabbed soap and rifle and headed back for the cabin. I was turning blue.

Inside, I wrapped up in some toweling and moved close to the fire to get dry. I turned to Henry and held the soap out to him.

"You're next, Indian." My teeth were chattering so I could hardly talk.

He stared at me, wide-eyed. "You're crazy," he stated.

I picked up my rifle, brought it to bear on him, and offered him the soap again. He took it reluctantly, mumbling in Pawnee or Ute or something, stripped off his buckskin shirt, leggings, and moccasins and headed for the door, wearing only the double-apron breechcloth which he favored over pants.

The scars on his chest and back were healing cleanly, but they looked big and ugly on his copper hide.

He was back in a minute or two, shivering and cursing and smelling of lye soap. I was getting dressed again.

"Who's next?" I asked.

The boy was already stripping down, eager and excited by the unusual diversion. I had to make him wait until I had my boots on so I could go out with him to stand by with the rifle. As it turned out, I also had to order him back when he had scrubbed. I believe he would have splashed around that pond for five or ten minutes if I had let him.

When I had him back inside by the fire, toweling himself off busily, Mr. Sneed took the soap and packed himself off to the pond for his turn, chuckling. He came back in chattering and puffing, with red cheeks and blue feet.

Then I nodded to Becky. "You too, missy." Her eyes grew large and she turned away. The boy bristled. "You turn your backs," he said.

So we turned our backs. When she headed for the door, wrapped in a blanket, and I picked up the rifle to follow, Jesse passed me and said, "No. You stay here." He had dressed and reloaded the Kentucky rifle. "All right," I said. "You go. And bring her right back. It's cold out there."

"I wondered if you had noticed that," Henry said.

What I had noticed was the way that blanket pulled around Becky when she went out the door. Between her everlasting angry tongue and that aloof manner of hers, like none of us or this place or the mountains themselves existed, I had never really got around to noticing what Becky looked like from the other side.

The Indian was grinning at me, that evil grin that made me feel like taking one more heathen scalp.

"Your face is turning red, paleface."

While the snow fell outside that night, we rested snug, warm, and clean in the firelit cabin and feasted on sizzling buffalo steaks, stewed wild berries, root pudding, and bannock biscuits.

As we sat back, full and relaxed and sipping hot coffee, I heard a stifled giggle and glanced around to find

77

Becky's eyes on me, and there were dimples in her cheeks. But even as I looked the dimples dissolved and the eyes went cold and angry again and she looked away.

"I thought for a minute the sun had come out," I said. "I guess I was wrong."

She looked at me like she wanted to say something, then turned away.

"You did look a mite peculiar comin' in from the pond," Mr. Sneed encouraged. "Didn't he, Becky?"

"I didn't notice," she muttered. Then she turned and blazed at me. "Why did you bring us here? I don't like it here."

That caught me tongue-tied. Where else would I have brought them? "I—I didn't have anyplace else to bring you," I apologized. Then Henry smirked and I realized I had backstepped like a total fool from the damned girl, and that made me mad. "You got someplace better to be?" I growled at her. ". . . That you can get to right now?"

"You just leave her alone," Jesse snapped.

"That's the best idea I've heard lately."

We woke to a world of muffled brilliance the next morning, a brand new world of blurred white terrain where the snow still fell unhindered.

Chapter Ten

Through that first snowfall and the bright days that followed it we stayed around close. We had enough meat for a while, and my thinking was that if anybody was out tracking in these hills, they would look sharpest right after the first snowfall. So I didn't want any trails showing around the valley where we were. At least not for a few days, until the unspoiled snow had become patterned with game trails enough to confuse the eye.

But after a while I was getting fidgety, and the meat was getting low. I decided to go hunting again. And this time, Henry said he was going, too.

It had been weeks since Henry had been on a horse, and his wound still pained him a little. Yet he saddled the paint and climbed aboard, and it didn't seem to bother him much when the horse tried to throw him off. He just rapped it between the ears with his rifle barrel, and it settled down in a hurry.

The gorge was flank-deep in powder snow, but the roan picked and pushed his way up through it with the paint following close behind. Soon we came out on top; two horses with pack braces brought up the rear. All around us lay the forest, dazzling white and deep green under a sky of pure azure. Ahead, to the west, was a high saddle pass between two snowbound peaks, and we headed for it.

There was game everywhere: rabbits exploding from snow burrows to go tumbling off through the drifts; dainty trails where lines of deer had passed; and far below us, off to the left now, threads of shadow in the snow where buffalo had wandered across a flat, pushing up drifts and mounds of snow as they went. I had note of their location, and we rode on. We climbed the saddleback at an angle, following the swales of shallow powder where we could, and came out on top to look across a vista out of a storybook. To the west the mountains went on and on, ridge after ragged ridge, brilliant in the high sunlight, snowclad slopes blinding as the sun caught new facets in their surfaces. It was a sight to lock in the mind, to conquer the memories of squalid places of the past, and to stand against the noticing of such places in the future.

I wanted to scout out the way to the trapping grounds Tad had spoken of, so we cut left to climb high on a ridge from which the ranges spread below us, angling up and back into the distant miles.

To the west, beyond several ridges and below the peaks of three great cones of mountain, was where it would be. It was a long way from where we sat, but I could see almost the whole trail from here.

Henry grunted and pointed off to the northwest. There, vivid but tiny in the sunlight, a file of Indians moved sedately along a slope, just under the crown of a ridge, heading south and west, angling away from us. Even at this distance, in the clear air, I could make out the colors of their buckskin garb, the sheen of the horses' coats, the reflection of sunlight on a naked lance. I counted fourteen, all men. Two or three carried guns, and the rest were armed with bows, lances, and axes.

"Cheyenne," Henry said. "Hunting party."

We watched until the procession disappeared around a shoulder of mountain. When they were gone, we turned and set off across slope, around the brow of the ridge, moving south.

That evening in a high meadow, we found elk, and just before dark Henry's shot dropped a huge bull at the foot of a granite outcropping. It was full dark and fiercely cold before we got the meat dressed and packed, so we found a sheltered thin area for the horses to graze and made camp right where we were.

Roasting fresh meat over a fire down under a cedar-hung shelf, I asked the Indian, "Henry, how come you're here?"

"Where?"

"Here. How come you're still hanging around? You're mostly mended now, and I'm not keeping you."

He didn't say anything, just sliced off some meat and chewed on it. So after a while I asked him again, "Why aren't you off looking for those Utes you picked up with? You can go when you want."

"I don't know where they are," he said, and it sounded more like he didn't care where they were.

"Well, then, how about those Cheyenne we saw to-day? You could find them."

"Phaw!" he spat. "Ride right up on a bunch of cut-fingers, would I. White-eyes, what you don't know about the wild people is just about everything there is to know. They'd have my scalp as quick as they'd have yours. I'm Pawnee, remember?"

"I thought you'd decided to be a Ute," I said, but he didn't have any comment on that.

After a while he asked, "Havin' me around make you nervous, does it?"

I couldn't rightly say it didn't, so I didn't. "I was just wondering why you're still here, that's all."

He looked up from the fire, and those Indian eyes weren't giving away any secrets. Then that devil grin spread across his face.

"I can give you several answers," he said, "and you can take your pick. Maybe I'm curious what you're going to do next. So far everything I've seen you do has been at least peculiar. Or maybe I just don't have anywhere else to go. And maybe those aren't the reasons at all. Maybe there's another reason."

"What other reason are you talking about?"

"I already told you that once before, white-eyes. You just think about it."

That was all he had to say, and thinking about it didn't shed any light on the matter.

The next morning we angled east, downslope, and detoured several miles around a crag to come to where we had spotted buffalo tracks. They were there, great dark shaggy brutes, bulling the snow aside effortlessly to get at the tender grass beneath. We picked out a fat old bull away from the herd, and I put a ball through his heart. A few of the others looked up stupidly when he fell, then went back to their grazing. Only when we rode down to get him did they move away.

With all our animals heavy laden, it was evening again when we dropped down through the gorge and headed back across the meadow to the cabin. Jesse was at the corral, rifle in hand, to meet us, and Becky met us at the door with a rare smile and the smell of fresh-baked biscuit. She was, I thought, a very pretty little girl.

It took a day to get the meat cut and hung and start jerking some of it. We were set for the winter now. Everything we needed was at hand. But come spring we would be moving, trying for some point of civilization, and we should have a stake. There was one good way to get it.

"When the next snow falls," I told them, "I will go to the three peaks to trap."

Then, on impulse, I packed a load of jerked meat in canvas, slung it behind a saddle and headed out and up the mountain, quartering back toward the top of the sentinel rock. Partway up I heard sound behind me and saw Henry following, on the paint.

"Offering to the spirits?" He asked as he came up.

"Offering to a boot track or a bear," I said. We rode on upward and came at last to the swale below the pinnacle or rock, tied the horses, and went on afoot. Coming out above the ledge I stopped and looked around. Shallow snow covered the shelf leading out to the head of the great stone. There were fresh tracks in it. Boot tracks.

"You were tellin' the truth," Henry said, quietly.

The tracks came down from the peak behind and led to the very edge of the precipice. The snow there was packed and scuffled where someone had stood around for a while. Then the tracks went back, leading past our position, on up the mountainside again. We followed them for a way, until they entered a great field of broken, upright slabs and spires on the mountainside where we lost them.

"Someone is holing up back in there," I said, pointing. "And he wears white man's boots. And whoever he is, he's hungry."

Henry nodded. The sign was all around. Roots had been dug, bark stripped from winter-bare branches, shoots pulled from the little patches of soil among the rocks. Some deadfall wood had been broken up and dragged away. There was in the evidences a great sadness. Here was sheer, mindless desperation without logic or reason. The feeling was akin to something I had felt just for an instant, back there by the creek, when I had shot a savage Indian from his saddle and then had looked around, moments later, to find that same Indian on his knees trying to reload his gun to kill me.

"It makes no sense," Henry was saying. The Indian's awe at madness was in his voice. "Just no sense at all."

"Maybe it does," I told him. "Just a little."

We left the jerked meat there where the tracks entered the rocks and some flint and steel with it, and Henry took his best blanket off his shoulders, folded it, and laid it there, too.

There was nothing more we could see to do, so we went back to the horses and started home. The sky around us was hazing over, and a new cold wind had sprung up around the peaks. Henry was shivering a little in the cold.

"You need that blanket," I told him.

"Not as bad as he does."

By the time we got back to the cabin and put the horses into shelter, the haze had deepened into a grey overcast, and winter's mantle was lowering again over the mountains. It was getting ready to snow again.

The cabin was warm, and the thought of those cold mountains to the west was not inviting. But I would need that stake come spring, and now was the time.

"If I ride out of here ahead of the snow," I told Mr. Sneed, "my trail will be covered. Nobody will follow it back here, or to where I'll be."

Becky was over in the corner, stitching softened deerhide with needle and thread from the packs. She had watched Henry sew hides, and had begun working on them herself to while the time. "You're going away?" she asked now. It was the first time she had spoken to me in days.

"There is a place west of here where I can trap. That's what I came here for."

"That's senseless," she said crossly. "You just want to

84

go off and leave us alone."

"Why would I do that?" I wondered, and saw Mr. Sneed shaking his head.

"Because we are a responsibility to you and we're all going to die here and you don't want to stay where you belong and take care of us."

It was so unfair it hurt, and so unexpected it left me speechless for a moment. I looked at the others. Mr. Sneed said, "Becky, there's no call to talk that way. We would have died out there if he hadn't found us."

Henry scowled, muttered, "Squaw talk," and went outside.

"You're well provisioned here," I told them. "There's wood for the fire and food to eat, and it's as safe a place as any. When I come back we'll see how the passes look, then maybe we can get to Santa Fe or someplace."

"You won't come back," the girl said, and now the cold anger in her voice was a hot anger, spilling into her eyes. "You'll just die out there in the cold, and we'll die here. You don't care, do you?"

"Of course I care, but I came here to trap, not to sit all winter being snapped at by a sour-talking she-bitch that can't find a decent word to say to anybody. If you can't be pleasant why don't you just shut up."

"Here," Mr. Sneed said, alarmed, and Jesse frowned and started to get to his feet, glaring at me. But the girl just stared at me a moment and went back to her stitching.

"Go ahead, then," she spat. "It makes no difference to me what you do."

It was decided. I would leave at first light.

With dark, the wind slacked off and the snow began to fall, trickling down on us, feather-light and dancing. I was out checking the horses for the night when the voice came again. Strong and deep, resonant and eloquent, seeming to come from heaven itself, the spirit voice descended with the snow over the dark, hushed valley.

"Blessed be he that considereth the poor: the Lord will deliver him in time of trouble."

I moved back from the corral shelter and looked around, then tried to look up to the top of the great rock, but there was nothing except the mute snow-flakes descending around me.

"The Lord will preserve him, and keep him alive; and he shall be blessed upon the earth; and thou wilt not deliver him unto the will of his enemies."

There was a blush of firelight on the falling snow, and the others were coming out of the cabin. They stood there outside the door, bunched together, looking around with frightened eyes. The voice went on, deep and warm with a comforting tone to it:

"The Lord will strengthen him upon the bed of languishing; thou wilt make all his bed in sickness."

". . . Lord, be merciful unto me; heal my soul; for I have sinned. . . ." It trailed off into the silence of the night and the falling snow. We waited, but there was nothing more.

Back in the cabin, no one said anything for a while. Henry sat cross-legged on a robe by the fire, thinking his own Indian thoughts, and the boy kept darting glances around here and there and kept the Kentucky rifle close at hand. As for Becky, her eyes were shining with the light of a strangeness propounded, a mystery unsolved. For a time she was shaken from whatever angry world she lived in.

As I sat pondering the strange voice high up on the rock, Henry's earlier remarks came back to me. Something about a "death wind" and "a ghost who walks" was what he had said. Thinking about his words, I asked him what he had meant.

"The Deathwind," Henry said, "is a legend held true by many tribes since long before my grandfather's time. A white man, a lone woodsman from beyond the land of the big lakes, swore vengeance upon all redmen and went out across the land seeking us, hunting down our bravest men, and declaring war on our warriors.

"Wild as the forests, strong in his hatred, and crafty in his determination, he succeeded fearfully well. No living redman has ever seen him or if he has, he did not live to tell of it. This white man roamed the woodlands and penetrated the cold prairies as far westward as the great peaks. And where he went, the people died. His long rifle did not miss. And though warriors of many tribes have sought him, he could not be found, except by those who found him and never returned.

"With time he became more than a man in the minds of our people. He became the most fearsome of spirits, and the mention of his name, Deathwind, could panic any village.

"No one has ever seen him, but they have heard him. When the Deathwind comes, he announces himself, his voice clear in the night, echoing through dark forest. His words are in the white tongue. But the words are of no matter. It is the voice that chills the marrow in the stoutest warrior's bones. That voice comes with the wind in the night and it is the wind of death.

"For my people, that terrible voice has become, with the growing of legend, exactly what our ancestors named him—the wind of death, Deathwind. Though he, by now, is dead, his spirit lives still, and it is a most fearsome spirit. A man might seek the voices of the Inti; he might even stand erect to hear the words of Wakan-Tonka, whom all tribes know. But no man can stand against the voice of the Deathwind. Of all the spirits that haunt the dreams of our people, he is the most terrible, for he had once been a man."

Henry's remarks left me, once again, with an uneasy feeling. I had never put much stock in the Indians' tales of spirits and ghosts. At least, not taken literally. But stripped of the restraints of language, the redman's superstitions were something more than just stories to widen the eye and raise the hackles. There was a sense woven through them, a feeling that, once felt, seeped into the mountains and the land and became a part of them. A feeling. . . .

I thought of Pastor Goodwin, that timid, pragmatic, kindhearted soul, gone with the captain's expedition. Vanished—like he had never been there at all. Just for a moment I had thought that, somehow, the voice on the mountaintop might be his. But that spirit voice was not the voice of the little man who had tended our souls along the trail toward the Shining Mountains. There was no comparison.

I slept with the mystery of it crowding through my dreams.

By the light of a snow-filled dawn I saddled the roan, put pack saddles and gear on the black and two others, and headed west in a muffled world to find my winter's fortune.

Chapter Eleven

Back East the story is that free trapping in the high mountains is a glamorous business. They make it a glorious adventure, a work to inspire a man to the noblest eminences of spirit.

"The free trappers possess," some writer had said, "the most formidable skill of their time, the noblest unfettered spirit that mankind has yet achieved."

All of that is wrong.

Trapping for hides in the Stony Mountains is hard, grueling, backbreaking work fit for no man with an ounce of good sense. In the weeks I spent alone in the solitude of the three peaks, I worked harder than I had ever worked before and suffered torments I would not have imagined. Cold meals in bitter, fireless camps were my constant fare, and frostbite my only companion. It was a constant struggle to protect the horses, work the miles of trap lines, break ice for water, find deadfall wood for an occasional fire when I lost the feeling in my toes and fingers—and a constant need for watching every backtrail, every place of concealment, every rock and snow-topped bush.

There were always wolves. They moved in around each camp I made, brave and determined, seeking a single chance to steal a morsel of food or bring down a strayed horse. I got so I knew some of them by sight, and had pet names for them, names I hurled at them along with chunks of ice when they ventured too close, their yellow eyes baleful in the grey dawn of high-country winter. Only once did I shoot at them, when a hunting pack surrounded my herd and tried to cut out a single horse. I picked a big, grey patriarch with a battle-scarred snout and shot him dead. After that they kept their distances for a while.

A hundred times I went over in my mind all the things I had been told or had read about how to set traps, how to lay out a line, where to cut a beaver slide; the use of scent from the musk glands of a beaver to hide the scent of human passage, and how to hide a trap in icy water at the foot of a bend, or mask it with snow on a trail. I caught beaver. By any standards I did well. After the first few tries I seldom came in empty-handed, and added to my work was the cold, foul job of preparing the plew for packing. Green hides had to be cured right or they would sour before they got to market.

In addition to the beaver, I caught muskrat and otter and an occasional fox, along with snowy weasels and two badgers out unseasonably in the snow. I had traps robbed, sometimes by wolves and twice by something I never could identify. But where a trap went robbed or bare, two others produced plew for me, and the packs mounted.

It snowed, and snowed again, and the weather went from cold to bitter. Some days I felt I would never be warm again. But I kept at it though my muscles ached through the stinging cold and my beard came in full and bristly.

I shot two buffalo during those weeks — or months — and one of them came back in death to almost kill me. It was a big, grizzled bull, breaking cover for winter grass. I killed him with a shot in the neck and skinned him out, then cut off what meat I could handle and packed it back to camp in the heavy skin.

I had a fire that evening and roasted the fresh hump meat, then spent a while scraping the hide. It was too cold by dark to do it right, however, and I was too tired to continue, so I turned in to wait for morning. In the middle of the night I awoke shivering. The sky was clear, and a new north wind was shipping down the mountains into the valley. The green hide lay close at hand so I pulled it near and rolled up in it, blankets, robes and all, and went back to sleep.

When I woke up again I was trapped. The green hide had frozen solid, and I was helpless inside it, bundled up like a caterpillar in a cocoon. Humiliation set in before fear. Like the greenest greenhorn, I was trapped by my own incompetence. Then as I struggled I began to realize how critical the situation was. I could hardly move. Lying on my side, arms up before me, I was fixed in position with that frozen hide clamped hard around me.

I began to work at it, and, slowly, the robe crackling and protesting, I worked both arms out straight, then began levering aside. Sweat was streaming down my face and I could feel my tendons crack as I applied every ounce of strength in the awkward position. But slowly, ponderously, the heavy robe loosened. It was near an hour before I finally struggled free, wheezing and exhausted. I didn't get much work done the rest of that morning.

Finally there came a clear, ice-bright day when the sun was up an hour after I was and the sky was still light with evening when I finished my work and crawled into the blankets, dead-tired, gaunt, and hard at the edges. And within a few days there were noon-time rivulets on the snow fields, and I could hear the faint thunder of avalanches here and there in the mountains. It was time to go home.

The mountains have a way of changing people to fit them, if those people survive long enough. When I came down from the three peaks, through the valleys of pine and granite and finally headed up through that saddleback swale toward home, I knew I was not the same person who had headed out from there with winter's second snow falling on me. Sometime in those cold, hard days I had passed my twentieth birthday. I had weathered. My muscles had grown hard, and I had no extra flesh on me anywhere. And somehow, it seemed, I rode a little taller in the saddle than before.

But it was more than that. Most of the weathering had been inside. You learn things in the high mountains, things about yourself and the world around you. And if you listen when the mountains speak, they have a way of filling in all the hollow places inside you, of answering the unanswered questions, of helping you know how things are and why they are that way.

When I reached the bottom of the gorge, the boy, Jesse, was there with his Kentucky rifle, and for a long moment he kept me covered before recognition dawned. Then he lowered it and came forward, his eyes on the pack-laden animals behind me but mostly on me. I must have been a sight to him, swathed in rawhide breeches and rough shirt, bundled in a bone-tied buffalo coat, a mass of rawhide, fur and whiskers atop a shaggy red-grey horse.

"You are older," he said finally, and I gave him a nod.

"So you are, Jesse. How are things here?"

"Fine. We're all right. Saw Indians the other day, way out there on that ridge line, but they went away."

Henry was waiting by the corral, looking healed and fit and wilder than ever in a beaded shirt of a soft buckskin. He favored me with a gaze of mock amazement, then came forward.

"You look like a pile of dead carcasses," he said.

The mocking faded when he looked over the hides I had brought out. "Four packs!" he said, and whistled.

"Three and a part," I said. "Almost four."

"Good plew," he admitted, thumbing up a few of the stiff pelts.

Then I saw Becky at the cabin door, and I knew for sure winter had brought some changes. She was wearing an Indian-style dress of soft doeskin and the heavy old coat thrown over it didn't hide the girl underneath. She looked at me solemnly for a moment. Then the frown crumpled, and she ran out and threw her arms around my neck, standing on tiptoe to reach me.

"You're back!" she told me. Then she backed off and made a wry face. Without another word she turned, ran back to the cabin and came back carrying a bar of soap. She handed it to me, pointed toward the lower pond and said, "Your turn."

It was almost a pleasure. I shed thirty pounds of clothing and then set to with that soap and shed almost that much grime, and when I came stomping into the cabin, sacking wrapped around my waist and my bare skin blue with the cold, there was a warm fire going, muslin to dry myself and a fine new suit of buckskin clothes which someone must have worked on all winter.

The shirt was tight through the shoulders and short in the sleeves, and the leggings were too short, but I was delighted with them. The buckskin was soft and had the scent of pine smoke about it.

As I finished dressing Becky came back into the cabin and looked at me, frowning.

"They're too small," she said. "How can they be too small? I made them a lot bigger than Han-Ra-Hay's."

"You made his, too?"

"Well, I couldn't just sit here all winter and do nothing. Besides, Grandfather told me to."

"Well, I like these very much, and they are just right. Are you still mad at me?"

"For going away? Yes. But at least you came back. I didn't think you would."

"And you cared?"

"Who else is going to get us out of here? That Indian? Of course I cared."

The old mulehide boots I had worn since I left Independence with Captain Mellett's crew were wrecked. They looked and felt shameful, matched up with my new buckskins.

Becky put her hands on his hips. "You'll need moccasins, I guess. I'll make them, but I'll have to measure your feet first."

I couldn't get over the change in her. The old anger was still there, but there was an acceptance along with it now, as though some of the old hard shell had melted away. I found I had to concentrate furiously to keep from thinking about what it might be like if it all did.

Mr. Sneed came trudging in from somewhere all apple-cheeked, tough, and fit. He looked younger, and he looked downright happy. And I was glad to see him. I was glad to see all of them. I was even glad, heaven help me, to see that Indian. It was the first time in my life I had ever really come home.

Of course, there was a fly in the ointment, and it was me. When I looked at Becky it shamed me what I found in my own mind. It had been a long winter, but I had no call to have such feelings, and I knew it. I vowed right then, with cold determination, that the stallion cavorting inside me must be hobbled and check-reined right now — and stay that way. I had no call, none at all, to let that long winter end.

Around a fire that evening we talked, laughed, compared notes, and generally got acquainted. It occurred to me that it was really the first time I had tried to get to know any of them, including the Indian.

They had changed since I had been away. So had I.

I asked about the Indians they had seen, two days before. "Do you think they saw you?"

"No." Jesse stated flatly. "They just showed on that ridge up there, then they went away."

Henry was lighting a pipe and looked up from it. "They saw us," he said. "They'll be curious, and they'll be back."

"Who were they? Could you tell?"

"Cheyenne. There were only three in the party or maybe four. They'll be back. I've been watching."

From the looks that Becky and Jesse gave him it was obvious he hadn't shared his concern, and I chalked up another mark in his favor.

"You're starting to think like a white man, Henry."

"You're just starting to understand Indian thinking, Ran-Da-Hay," he answered flatly.

It was good to be home. I found I was considering this place as home, and the thought came easily and had a comfortable way about it.

Jesse was full of bubbling talk about his shooting—he was getting pretty good, he said, and Henry nodded—about the horses, which had wintered well, and about everything in general. Becky was like a discovered gem, quick and pretty, making the wanderer feel welcome at home. She would be a fine woman some day—I got busy thinking about something else.

And Henry, well, his wounds had healed, and I guess mine had, too. The redskin and I were at peace as of now.

"You know, the passes will be open soon," I said.

"Then we will go. There will be enough of us to drive the horses to Santa Fe."

"Yes, we will go." Henry's gaze was level. "You including me in?"

"I hadn't thought otherwise. Will you go with us?"

"I guess so. I haven't seen Santa Fe."

"Then it's settled. We've got enough furs out there to see us all to wherever we're going from there."

I should not have said that. The thought of going our own obscure ways, of parting at Santa Fe, was a cloud on the warmth of the cabin, and I realized with a pang that none of them except me had anyplace particular to go from here.

Well, we would just have to face that when we came to it. I had one main goal for my part, and that was to get the remainder of Captain Mellett's horses back to civilization, to his heirs, whomever they might be. Beyond that I had no very clear intent.

It may be a feminine credo that a lapse in the conversation is a vacuum best filled with food. At any rate, that was when Becky brought out the pie. It was a concoction of who knows what, looking like moist hard bread in gravy and smelling of spices, and it tasted like apple pie.

"Our mother used to make it," was the only explanation she offered.

Jesse added, "She made it for us when we ran out of apples."

Henry was entranced. He dug into the pie, demolished it and called for seconds until there was no more. "All winter long you've known how to make that," he accused Becky, "and you wait until now to bring it out."

She glanced at Henry, then at me.

"I was waiting," she said. "This surprise was not for any who threatens squaws."

When I went out a little later, in the dark of evening, Mr. Sneed followed me, and we stood for a while in the dark snow meadow watching the stars break out of holes in the clouds.

"You notice about Becky," he said after a bit.

"Yes, I noticed. What's happened, Mr. Sneed?"

"Well, you know, she's been awful unhappy. When their daddy felt the need to move, we all just packed up and moved."

"Yes, you told me."

"Well, everything just happened too fast then for Becky. Mind you, she's of an age that's awful important to a young girl. Just come of age, you might say, and bad things that happen then can be fearful bad. I recollect her mother at the same age, and her grandmother too, comes to that, and I swear there's no understanding of just how powerful a young girl can feel what goes on around her.

"Anyway, she was just at that age — young men startin' to admire and all — and she lost her mother. It like to broke her up for sure. And then right on top of that her pa, he just couldn't be at peace there, and he had to move on.

"Jesse now, to him it was all a big adventure. The excitement of moving kind of eased his misery about his mother. But with Becky it was different. I guess it seemed like she was trying to hang on to all she had left in her young life, and up comes life and takes it away from her. Home, friends her age, the coming of growing up time that she'd looked forward to in the place she knew.

"When we packed that wagon and moved on, it just like to broke her heart. She pined, son, she surely did, and none could console her."

I didn't know what to say, so I didn't say anything. After a while he went on.

97

"All those long miles, and all that lonesome. She just wasn't there with us, Randy, not in her mind. All that long way she was mourning.

"And then when those men came—Becky was right there not an arm's length from her pa when he went down. Well, she just kind of exploded, don't you know. I believe she had to either get mad or go mad, and she's too strong a girl to do the second.

"I swear it took a lot of mad to save that child, but she called it forth and did it. Sorta like, well, like the only thing she had to hang on to was being angry."

"But not anymore," I allowed.

"No," he said. "Not anymore. Han-Ra-Hay saw to that."

I started. "Mr. Sneed, that Indian, he didn't—"

"No, son, nothin' like that there. No, it was like this: After a few days of deep snow, all of us in that little cabin 'cept when we had to go out, it looked like one of two things was gonna happen. Either three of us was gonna move out or one of us was, and I swear I was about ready for it to be that girl.

"Then one mornin' she lit after Han-Ra-Hay. No special reason, just he was where she happened to be lookin' when her tongue started up. Well, he took it about as long as he could. Then he just kicked her feet out from under her, and she sat plop down right there in the middle of the floor.

"Then he pulled that old big knife of his and offered to notch her ears for her if she didn't hush up. Said he'd known squaws traded off to the Osage for talkin' half as much."

I just stood there, filled with the vision he had called up. That furious little girl dumped unceremoniously on the floor and lectured to on etiquette by a savage with a knife. My first instinct was to get mad, but then it struck me funny, and I started to laugh.

Mr. Sneed nodded. "You see? That's what happened. All of a sudden Becky just bust out laughing, and she's been mostly all right since."

"Can't say as much for Han-Ra-Hay," he added. "Don't believe he ever expected to be laughed at." He chuckled.

The stars were full out now, the clouds breaking up. They sparkled up there, like Becky's eyes. Not the Becky I had found lost on the cold shoulder of a mountain, but the Becky who had blended stale flour, sugar and spices to make apple pie. Mr. Sneed was studying me, slant-wise.

"You'll remember your word, son?"

"Yes, sir. I'll remember my word."

In the bright morning I pulled on my heavy coat and went outside to stand a while before the cabin, stretching and yawning, looking out over the valley. Henry and Mr. Sneed were already out, tending to the horses, and I could hear Becky stirring about inside, building up the fire, splashing water into the coffee pot.

Snow still lay on the valley floor, but it was hollow at the bottom, resting on a skim-ice crust, and the holes in it showed new life. Along the bottom of the great standing altar stone, the winter's drift had thawed back from the rock to leave a cleft running ground-deep behind the sharp, transparent comb of ice. And the great stone stood there, untouched by winter or spring, untouchable by the puny seasons, disdaining all before it with equal indifference.

I let my eyes travel at ease to the top, and made out the hairline edge of the crust of snow up there on the pinnacle. Henry came up as I was looking there and said in that soft voice, "I've taken food up there. Seen tracks, but nothing more."

"He should come down," I said. "He should go with

us to Santa Fe."

All Henry said was, "I doubt if he knows we're here."

"Then let's tell him."

Becky had breakfast on when we went in, and I packed a haunch of venison, some biscuits, and some ground coffee. Later Henry and I saddled up and headed for the gorge.

Up the mountainside there were tender traces of green all around, poking bravely through the crusted snow, showing around the edges of ice slopes, pushing up through white-mantled rocks. The air was still brittle, but there were beads on the limbs of the aspen trees and the vibrance of spring in the pines.

When we walked out on the shrouded pinnacle I immediately saw boot tracks, some fresh, some as old as the last snow. But no recent ones approached near the edge.

We climbed up to the maze of rock where we had left that first offering and put the package there as before. Then I stepped up on an outcrop and cupped my hands to my mouth.

"You there! Hello! There's food here, and we want to talk! We are friends!"

The echoes were long in coming from the peaks around, but they were the only answer. I tried again.

"Come out and talk! We are your friends! We mean you no harm!"

There were only the echoes, ringing in the icy stillness of the morning, and Henry looked around nervously. "You had better stop."

We waited there a while, but nothing happened. Whoever was up there either didn't hear or didn't want to answer. Finally we gave up.

We were halfway down the mountain when the bear attacked.

Chapter Twelve

He was a big old silvertip with all the fat slewed off him by hibernation. He was gaunt, rangy, and bad-tempered, and he wasted no time on formalities. He was standing there when we came around an outcrop, and when he saw us he came for us.

Before I could bring the Hawken up, he was rearing over me, forepaws up and those little pig eyes a yard from my face. He slashed downward as the terror-stricken roan sidestepped. A paw the size of a deer's haunch, and sprouting claws like spikes, slammed into my shoulder and slapped me backward out of the saddle. The roan reared and plunged away. I had a sideways glimpse of Henry clinging to the paint as it pitched and danced up the slope. I hit the ground hard, flat on my back.

. . . And just lay there. I knew I should move, and I told myself that, but nothing happened. I just lay there and began hurting.

The bear was down on all fours again, diverted for a moment by the racket Henry's horse was making up the slope. I had hung onto the rifle, but I couldn't get my arm to work to bring it up. The bear swung around, slowly like a grumpy old man, and his eyes fixed on me just about the time I managed to move my left leg. The motion annoyed him. He growled and came forward a step, then reared again. From where I lay, he towered treetop-tall, and ugly, black lips twisted back from great yellow fangs with a growl rumbling up through him.

Henry's rifle cracked from up-slope someplace, and I saw dust erupt from the monster's side just below an upraised arm. The bear roared and shook his head, then focused on me again, and as I finally got the rifle moving I knew it was too late. Sunlight filtering through dark boughs beyond that shaggy head was the last thing that I would see.

I don't know what prompted the roan to turn back. Maybe there was a spark of concern in his horse brain; more likely he was just fighting mad. But suddenly he was there, empty saddle trappings swinging around him, teeth bared and his ears laid back, rearing high beside the bear. Forefeet lashed out like mill pistons, and he screamed a battle cry that went clear back to his wild ancestors on the steppes.

The bear no more than turned his head when a slashing hoof thudded into him, staggering him. Another caught him across the nose, and he wailed like a lost baby, blood gushing from his face. He turned on the maddened horse and lashed out at it with a massive paw. In that time I brought the Hawken up one-handed and fired it into his exposed chest.

He swung back toward me, tormented and furious, roaring and slinging blood as he turned. Henry's French rifle boomed again, closer up. Far away down the mountainside I heard someone shout.

The roan wheeled and charged again, this time headlong with all the power of those driving legs, and hit the grizzly with a shoulder, bowling it over. The horse went down, too, from the force of the blow, but was up again in an instant. Then rearing tall above the struggling brute, it brought both forefeet down together with all its weight behind them. They thudded into the bear's side, smashing it to the ground. Again and again the red horse reared and struck, and the sound of those hoofs was like an axe hitting a side of meat.

The shock of the fall was wearing off, and I pulled myself up against a cedar stump and started reloading the Hawken rifle. I didn't need it again though. The roan was pummeling a carcass. The bear was dead.

Finally the horse backed off, lathered and wild-eyed, to stand trembling and pawing a few feet away. Its ears were still back but its terrible rage was dissipating. It pawed nervously at the icy ground with feet that were splattered to the knee with blood. Coming down through the trees, Henry made a wide circle around the roan and its kill.

My legs felt weak and shaky. I made it over to a rock and sat down. Henry tied the paint back a ways and came up to join me there. It would be a while before the roan could be calmed enough to ride, but I was in no hurry.

My heavy buffalo coat was ripped across the shoulder where the bear had caught me with that first slap. A flap of woolly hide as big as a man's hand hung from it, torn loose by massive claws. I was bleeding a little, but the heavy coat had absorbed most of the impact. I would have a nasty bruise on the shoulder and maybe some more on the back and one leg, but nothing was broken. As soon as the roan would allow it, Henry pulled his knife and matter-of-factly set about skinning the bear.

When we came down off the mountain all the horses were shut up in the corral and the cabin was closed tight with rifles protruding all around. As we came into clear view, one of the rifles pulled in, the door swung open, and Jesse came out to meet us.

"We heard shooting up there," he started, then his eyes lit on the bear hide, head intact, folded behind Henry's saddle. "Oh," he said, backing off a step.

Becky came out, and they both had to hear all about it. And when we got around to unsaddling the horses, my roan got more attention than he was used to. An angry horse is a formidable fighter any way you look at it. But a horse that will jump a grizzly—and stomp it into the ground—is something special.

In the cabin Henry and I looked around with amazement and delight.

Chinks had been knocked out of the walls on the three open sides and all the extra rifles were propped there, loaded and primed, giving the rough little cabin the appearance of a fort.

"We thought Indians had got you," Mr. Sneed explained apologetically. "We didn't know what else to do."

Henry grinned. "You did just right. No Indian in his right mind would have ridden up on this place with all those guns poking out."

Becky was fussing over the blood on my shoulder, so I pulled off coat and shirt and sat down. I don't know whether she was more upset about the rips in the buckskin shirt or the rips in me, but she set about patching up both of us right away. Jesse and Mr. Sneed went off to help Henry with the bear hide, and I headed for the coffee pot.

For the next three days, off and on, Henry worked over that bear hide. Spreading it fur down on a smooth rock he stretched and pegged it, then spent most of a day scraping every particle of flesh and membrane from the hide. In the evening he spread crushed bark over it and a thick layer of mushy snow over that, and let it soak. The next morning he cracked off the ice and scraped some more, then poured hot water over it and scraped again. Next he layered it deep in wet wood ash and let that soak. Then he scraped again, took it up, and worked it for hours, pulling and stretching with his hands, softening the leather. When it was finally done to his satisfaction he trimmed the edges here and there, sewed up the rends where the horse's hoofs had broken through, and donned it like a hooded robe.

We were out in front of the cabin when he tried it on, and it was a sight to behold. The head skin, bear-face features gnarled and evil-looking, fit over the crown of his head like a cowl with the black nose resting at the peak of his forehead. Below this crown of savage majesty the great fur robe flowed down across his shoulders, heavy and draped, to hang in rounds and frays of grey-gold fur just about the tops of his beaded moccasins. Closing it at the throat with a bone hasp, he postured before us, features grave, arms spread under the cloak so that it hung full round behind him, then arms down and one side of the robe thrown back over his shoulder with a flourish. Prancing there in the high sunlight, the empty bear face over his brow, the great fur cape swirling heavily as he moved, he was the epitome of the noble savage, a wild, magnificent aborigine in the full glory of new garb.

He did a few Indian dance steps, feet thudding the drying earth and hands spread wide, beads and raven braids flashing sunlight, then swirled full around, thunked his moccasined heels together and performed a stiff bow to Becky.

"I, madame, am the king of England."

She giggled and clapped in delight. Jesse laughed aloud, then pulled his young face straight again. "You look more like an overgrown badger," he said solemnly. Mr. Sneed was like to choked to death.

In those bright days, as patches of new green grew among the last crusts of snow, we worked and talked and tended the horses. We were all dressed in buckskin now, all wearing moccasins, and all looking just about as wild as Henry. All except Becky. She wore doeskin and moccasins and wore them like a young lady of quality. Or, maybe, with her gold hair braided tightly in long twin ropes, more like a viking princess.

All of this — the weather and Becky — caused me to have thoughts of spring. I was premature, however. Henry said we would have one more shot of winter, and he proved to be correct.

A week went by, and suddenly the balmy weather was gone. A fresh north wind whipped above the peaks, bringing with it haze and scudding icy clouds. It turned cold enough to singe the face with frostbite and drive freezing draughts through the rough-chinked walls.

The sky became darker and more bleak as two days passed, then three, and a wind like none I had seen through the long winter howled outside the cabin door.

We stayed close, going out reluctantly when we had to and coming in soon to the fire.

"What day is this?" Becky asked suddenly on the third afternoon.

"March, I think," I told her.

"But what day in March?" she insisted.

For the life of me, I didn't know and no one else seemed to care, but it seemed important to her so I creased my brow and put my chin in my hands for a few minutes, then said, "The twentieth. Today is the twentieth of March."

If I hoped to please her I was wrong. She sat down and stared at the wall, and her eyes began to moisten, then a tear trickled down her cheek. Henry had come in, and now he turned on me accusingly. "What did you do?" he demanded.

"Nothing — that I know of. I don't know."

Becky was still staring at the wall. "I'm sixteen," she said, and her voice sounded plaintive and desolate. "I have been sixteen for a whole week and didn't know it."

The snow that fell this time was a hard, grainy snow which ran along the icy ground in serrations ahead of the gusting wind. It was grey snow under a hard grey sky, lacking even the terrible charm of a midwinter blizzard.

"Colder than it ought to be," Henry commented.

Then it was gone, leaving behind a cheerless world of gloomy ice and grey mountains. As soon as it was passable outside Henry and I packed a large sack with food, including some pemmican of berries and bear meat, and headed out for the altar top. I was worried about the man on the mountain.

The precipice presented a vista of bleak grandeur to the eye. The air was clear under the hanging clouds and two grey ranges ran out together to blend at the high slopes and the edge of the earth, the clouds above and the mountains below, each as somber as the other.

The supplies we had left the last trip were still there, untouched. The haunch of venison had been nibbled at by birds and varmints, and their tracks were around it in the clean-swept snow, but no new human tracks were in sight. We stood there for a while, absorbing the testimony of the little bundle of unused food. Finally Henry took an audible breath and turned away.

"Deathwind has gone home."

That seemed to sum it up.

Deep inside me I felt a sense of loss. The man on the mountain had been a part of this place, as natural as the peaks around us, as fitting as the valley below, as proper in this place as the great cathedral rock from which his eloquence had rolled forth with the thunder—and floated downward with the falling feather snow.

Without looking at Henry I knew the Indian shared the feeling, the desolation, maybe even more than I. His roots were deeper in these mountains than mine could hope to be. We stood there for a long time, feeling the biting wind on our faces, backs to the mute unclaimed supplies, gazing out over the cold grey world.

"God, how I hate this place," I exclaimed suddenly, impulsively.

The Indian gave me a long, evaluating glance then turned away again so that his voice came from beyond the bearskin cowl.

"You lie, white-eyes. I think you love these mountains more than I."

"Let's go home, Henry." And home was just below us, a slap-up cabin in a hidden valley beneath cathedral rock.

Chapter Thirteen

The passes remained snowbound but they would be open soon. We worked and waited.

It was on a day when the sun rose high to burn through the chill in the air that the *tisi-tsi-ista*, whom Henry called cut-finger and I called Cheyenne, came upon us. Since the day when I brought a herd of horses and a bleeding Indian into this sheltered valley, I had used the north pass only once. At first I had avoided it intentionally because of the possibility of someone's snooping along the trail of the horse herd. Then we had adopted the west gorge, which was visible from the cabin, as our regular entrance and exit. The north pass, hidden almost at the foot of the cathedral rock, was left alone. It was by this route that the Cheyenne descended, and they were upon us almost before we knew they had come.

I was out by the corral with Mr. Sneed working on the fence, and Jesse was sitting on a rock watching. Becky was inside the cabin, and Henry had gone in to fetch the shovel when I turned around, and there they were.

There were seven of them in sight, tall and bright-garbed, astride blanketed mountain ponies, decked out in buckskins ornate with quills, bright feathers, and bits of colored stone. They had come around the foot of the altar stone and sat their horses in a line stretching from near the corner of the cabin to almost south of us.

When I turned and froze, Jesse turned, too, and I heard his gasp loud in the silence. Mr. Sneed turned and stared. They had made no sound at all.

Jesse was holding the Kentucky rifle, and as I saw his knuckles whiten I said, "No, Jesse. Don't move."

The Hawken was leaning nearby, but I dared not reach for it.

Three of them carried rifles; the others had arrows in their bows. But they weren't threatening us. They just looked. For a minute or more we stood like that, the only movement being the pawing of a horse. Then Henry came out of the house and found himself standing six feet from a Cheyenne warrior. And for once in his life he had no gun in his hand.

They looked at him, then back at me, and finally one of them, a big brave in the middle, raised a hand at arm's length and pointed toward me. He spoke in a voice that was haughty, grave and imperious—but not necessarily hostile. At my silence he turned to Henry, regarded him coolly and repeated the same phrases. Henry just stared back at him. I took a tentative step forward, and nothing overt occurred, so I took a couple more and said, "Who are they, Henry?"

He turned, and there was no emotion on his face or in his voice.

"They are Cheyenne. I don't understand their language except a few words."

He turned back to them, raised his hands, and made motions in swift, fluid sign, his fingers fairly dancing. They watched him intently. Then the chief, or whatever he was, laid his rifle across his lap and answered in equally fluent sign.

"They are a hunting party," Henry said. "They want to know who we are."

"Tell them our names, yours and mine, and say we're friends . . ." Then I remembered something Captain Mellett or old Rollo had said about the Cheyenne and I added, "Tell them we are guardians of a spirit place."

He threw me a puzzled glance, but went on with the hand language, paused to point to himself and say "Han-Ra-Hay," and to me, "Ran-Da-Hay," then made more sign. The silent warriors watched intently, their somber, savage faces impassive. It struck me that these were extraordinarily handsome people, with a measure of wild pride in the way they sat their horses and the way they looked us over.

When Henry stopped they talked among themselves for a moment, quietly. Then the one on the left nearest Henry pointed at him and said something with a hard, unfriendly sound to it. The chief raised a hand to hush him, then his hands spoke again.

"He says these are Ute names," Henry said, "and Utes are their enemies. He wants to know if we are Utes."

It was an inspiration then that helped me answer. Without pause I reached to my belt, untied the seasoned scalp which I still wore there, and raised it high. I said, "Ute. Uinay."

They seemed, if inscrutable faces can seem, skeptical but impressed. The chief said something, and the one on the far end, to my right, kneed his pony forward until he was beside me. He looked me over carefully, then reached out and took the scalp from my hand. He studied it, then raised it above him and said to the others, "Ute."

Henry said, "You've impressed them, Ran-Da-Hay. Uinay was considered a great warrior, and the Chey-

111

enne knew of him. Uinay took many Cheyenne scalps."

The chief was looking at Henry. Not taking his eyes off him as he pointed to the scalp his warrior held. "Uinay?" he asked.

Henry nodded, a single dip of the head. "Uinay."

Still riding the impulse I unbuckled the belt I wore and slid it off carefully. I held it up to the warrior so he could see the dented buckle, and I lied without a qualm. "Uinay," I said.

They talked that over among them; then the warrior handed the belt and scalp back to me and rode back to his place in the line.

Trying not to hurry and ignoring the Indians, I walked back to the fence, picked up my Hawken and cradled it across my left arm, then walked back until I stood directly in front of the chief.

Jesse sat like a rock, watching it all. He hadn't moved a muscle. Mr. Sneed leaned against the corral, relaxed—or so it appeared.

"Tell him this is our place that we keep for Deathwind, and that we welcome them to stop here if they come as friends. Offer them food and tobacco."

While Henry was telling them, I spoke again, not turning my head or raising my voice. "Becky, move as quietly as you can. Get a rifle and point it out the front wall. Let it show, but don't let them see you."

For a moment I didn't know if she had heard me. Then a rifle muzzle thrust out through an open chink, aimed straight at the nearest Cheyenne.

"Fine," I said. "Now, Mr. Sneed, walk into the cabin. Becky, the rest of them. All in front."

Another rifle appeared, then another, and another. It was impressive. A couple of Indians glanced around, and one grunted at the chief who glanced at the cabin then went back to watching Henry's hands with no sign of concern at all.

When Henry stopped, the chief made brief signs and pointed an accusing finger at his chest. Henry answered again with sign, then said, "He thinks maybe I am a Ute. I told him I am Pawnee." The chief was making more sign and Henry added, "He has nothing against the Pawnee."

A couple of them were eyeing the horses, those in the corral and the few out on the flat. I told Jesse, without looking around, "Jess, bring your gun to bear on the second one from the right. Don't shoot. Just point it at him politely."

I threw the chief what I hoped was a proud but friendly look, then said, "Becky, put one of those guns right on that nearest one's gizzard."

They didn't miss the motions of the gun barrels, and they stopped eyeing the horses that way.

"Henry," I said, "tell the chief we are mighty hunters and have plenty of meat, and invite them to stay for dinner."

He did and they talked about it, their voices low and sibilant in their strange, rhythmic tongue. One of them, a big brave with narrow eyes and a prominent nose, was objecting, looking more and more hostile. I brought the Hawken up so that it obviously was interested in him, and he subsided.

Finally the chief made a sign or two and slipped down off his horse. The others followed suit. Henry led them around to the lower pond, away from the cabin, and I went in to check the cabin. Becky's eyes were big and frightened, but she and her grandfather had those rifles lined up in workmanlike order. I told them to fix up a big dinner, as quickly as possible, and to let Mr. Sneed and Jesse bring it when it was done. No matter what, Becky was to stay in the cabin, out of sight.

She did fine. Within the hour we were sitting in a circle beside the lower pond, eating hot venison and biscuit, and drinking coffee. Me, seven wild Indians, and a half-tame one. And with Henry's sign language bridging the gaps, we were getting along very well.

The chief was called Tall Man Walking, and he was indeed a minor chief in his tribe. He was a distinguished-looking savage with some grey streaking his hair and a sure, quiet way about him. The big, feisty one with the narrow eyes was a younger warrior by the name of Red Leg, and the one who had inspected the Ute scalp was a stocky, broad-shouldered man called Slow Bear, who seemed always to have a spark of humor somewhere inside him. Indeed, I had the feeling that even if he decided to kill one of us he would do it in a good-natured way. Of them all, only Red Leg wore scalps at his belt.

Tall Man Walking wanted to know more about our claim that we lived in Deathwind's place, and I let Henry do the explaining since it was his hands and his story. They all watched in silence as the hands spoke, and the chief finally nodded, spoke to the others, then spoke by sign to Henry for a minute or two.

"He believes us," Henry said, relieved. "His grandfather lived for a time with the Hurons so he knows all about Deathwind, and he says some of his braves have heard his voice in these mountains before the last snows fell."

By the time the meal was done and Jesse brought pipes and tobacco, I had decided we were among friends. But I wasn't too sure about Red Leg. He seemed to have taken a personal interest in me and kept throwing that narrow-eyed glare my way as we ate.

"That one is feeling playful," Henry told me aside. "If he offers to make a bet with you, be careful about accepting." I was a little unclear about what he meant.

They had some news for us. Tall Man Walking said there were Utes in the area, come across the high peaks before the final snow, on a raiding expedition. He didn't know just where they were, but there were a lot of them. He held up the fingers of both hands, then closed them and held up six fingers. Then he drew the index fingers of both hands down and outward across his cheeks. That one was easy. The Utes were wearing war paint.

There were also other white men around, he said. He waved an arm in a wide arc south and east, then showed five fingers.

One of the Indians was admiring Henry's bearskin cloak, and Henry proudly pulled it around to show them the tattered side where the underskin showed clearly the rends and stitched gashes made by the horse's hoofs. As they looked on in wonder he sign-talked at great length, and they looked more and more impressed.

Suddenly I had a feeling Henry had gone too far. But they passed it by and went on to talk of other things.

At one point Tall Man Walking got a puzzled look on his face and signed a quick question to Henry, pointed at the cabin and then spread his hands and turned them palms down before us. The question bothered Henry.

"He wants to know why the ones in the cabin don't come out and join us," he said.

"Tell him that the men in the cabin do not wish to be unfriendly to our friends, but it is their duty to stay there and keep watch."

He told them. The chief puzzled it over for a moment, then signed back.

"He says, 'what are they watching for?' "

I looked sidelong at Tall Man Walking as I told him, "Say they are watching for Indians."

Henry hesitated, started to argue, then he grinned and told them.

It took a minute to soak in, and when it did Tall Man Walking favored me with a long, straight-faced appraisal, then smiled slightly and nodded. "*Tlinglit tsi-hya*," he said.

Henry told me, "That one I know. It means, 'true arrow.' If he was a Frenchman he would have said 'touche.' "

Three of them stood up and walked off to look around, and I started to get up to follow them but Henry motioned me to stay put. "Don't insult them. They'll look, but they won't take anything. That's one thing about Cheyenne. They don't steal." Nonetheless, he told Jesse to go and stand by the cabin and keep them away from there.

We talked some more with Tall Man Walking, about trails and hunting, about the winter and the spirit on the rock—every once in a while one or another of them would gaze long at the high crest of the rock above us, but they saw nothing there. Then I got up casually and walked across to see what Red Leg and his companions were looking at.

I found them at the corral, gazing at the horses there. When I came up, a small, wiry Indian I knew as Three Trees turned and said something to me, then repeated it in sign. I shrugged, and he tried again, more simply, making the sign for horse and another sign which I didn't recognize, then a swift chopping motion downward. He wanted to know which horse had killed the bear.

I point out the roan and said, "Roan horse." He looked pleased that we had communicated, then went back to looking at the horse. Red Leg, leaning on the top rail beside him, tried the words out. "Roan hoess," he said, savoring the sound of it.

After a moment he strode away to where the Indians' horses were picketed and came back leading his, a husky, vital mountain pony with good lines.

Red Leg planted himself in front of me and spoke in a loud voice, so I would understand. Pointed from his horse to me, then from the roan to himself, he said, "Trade — roan hoess!"

"No," I told him. "No trade. I thank you for your offer, but I'll not trade the roan horse."

The words meant nothing to him, but he understood. He looked crestfallen and a little angry. With an accusing glance he turned and led his horse back to the others and replaced the picket pin. Then he returned to the corral and stood again, gazing at the roan. After a fashion, I understood his feelings.

A little while later the Indians gathered around, Tall Man Walking said a few words that sounded like a formality, and they mounted up.

"Tell them we wish them much game and few enemies, Henry," I said. "Tell them we wish them good hunting."

He did so, and as they turned to leave Tall Man Walking smiled, raised his hand and led them away. They lined out down the valley toward the gorge. Red Leg was bringing up the rear, and as they rode away he turned for a long look back at the corral.

When they were gone Becky came out of the cabin and sat down on the rock by the door. "I thought they would never leave," she said.

Mr. Sneed asked Henry, "Will they come back, do you think?"

Henry shrugged. "Maybe, maybe not. You can't ever tell what an Indian is thinking."

Chapter Fourteen

We waited as the snow dulled and thinned all across the pasture. It still lay sparse through the woods, in the shadows of the conifers, but was diminishing. And we kept a sharp eye on the high peaks for sign of springtime creeping up from below.

Mr. Sneed was often with me when I worked the horses, and generally kept his own counsel. But as the land changed he seemed to change, too. Physically, during the months he had been in the valley, he had blossomed out from the bleak, defeated old man Tad Murphy had found into a spry and energetic specimen at the peak of life. He had a tough streak in him that showed now and then, and always surprised me. Like the time during the deep snows of that last storm when Jesse, frustrated by being too long cooped up had gone on a tear in that tight little cabin, sassing and aggravating everybody in general. It had gone on about as long as I was ready to stand for, and Henry — who was on a short fuse most of the time anyway — was about fed up. But neither of us solved the problem. The old man had been sitting quietly over in his corner, legs crossed and pipe smoldering. He put down his pipe, stood up, and caught Jesse by the back of the neck before the kid knew what was happening. He bent him

118

over and delivered a full-hand swat to his backside that would have made echoes if we'd been outside.

Whether from pain or sheer surprise, I don't know, but Jesse's mouth flew open and his eyes went wide. Then the old man picked the boy up by the collar and seat and said, "Henry, oblige me, will you?" The Indian opened the cabin door, and Mr. Sneed took Jesse out and pitched him into a drift. "Cool head never hurt a young'un," he said.

Once in a while he would talk, usually about the war. He hadn't seen much of it, really, but he had been a grown man when it was happening and understood more than the rest of us of what had happened. He'd had a younger brother hurt at Washington when the British stormed the place. And he had shaken hands once with Andy Jackson.

"Jackson is a westward man," he would say, and nod. "The prime folk back East, they don't think much of him. He ain't their kind.

"Not surprising politics is what they be in the States," he'd say. "We got two kinds of people running things, and they won't ever see eye to eye. They can't. They're different. One kind is the prime folk, them as stand firmly on the Atlantic shore and think like Englishmen. T'other is folk like most of us, with our backs to England and a country of our own to settle."

One time when he was talking on that way Henry said, "You're forgetting the third kind, Mr. Sneed. The ones that were already here." And Mr. Sneed looked at him with that mild expression and a twinkle in his eye and said, "Beg pardon, Han-Ra-Hay, I keep forgetting you ain't people."

Mr. Sneed always could go that Indian one better when he set his mind to it.

But mostly the old man kept his own counsel, and he never did talk about how the children lost their parents except one time. We were out in the meadow, he and I and Henry.

"Reuben was a good man," he said. "After I lost Mary, when I thought I'd never make it through another day, he and Julie took me into their house and shared their life with me."

It was much on his mind just then, for a bit later he said, "It hit Reuben terrible hard when Julie died. He just couldn't stay there anymore. You know, that's why we come west. I thought it was a hard time to pull little Becky up by the roots like that, just when the young men were startin' to notice her and all. But Reuben just couldn't stand being there where he and Julie had been. And it wasn't my place to say yea or nay to it. So we come."

I thought it had been hard for him, too, and said something of the sort.

He said, "Reckon I'd rather have stayed near Mary, God bless her soul. But I suppose as long as I'm where I can lend a hand to those children, I'm where Mary wants me to be."

With the sun getting warmer by the day, I was becoming fidgety. I judged the passes might be open, but now and again we could hear the rumble of an avalanche in the distance, and I didn't know enough about these mountains to be willing to take chances with them. None of us had been here long enough to see a thaw, but I knew I had seen places where I wouldn't want to be when the snow started sliding off those big slopes.

I needed to wait, but waiting also was making me nervous. Those Utes were out there someplace, and I had an unsettling feeling that Felix Briole and his bunch were, too. I wasn't too concerned about the Cheyenne. Those who had dropped in on us—all except maybe Red Leg, who wanted that roan horse so bad he could taste it—had seemed willing to leave us alone.

Through the long winter I hadn't worried much about hostile traffic of any kind. There wasn't any traffic. We couldn't move out, but neither was anyone very likely to move in. With the beginning of the spring thaw, though, anyone around would be traveling again. The trails were open. And when Red Leg showed up a second time, making another try to get himself that roan horse, that decided it. There was just getting to be too much traffic through this secret place of mine.

Red Leg came alone on his second visit, riding in from the north as they had come before, leading two extra horses. He wanted to talk business. With Henry handling the translations by sign, we talked. Red Leg had got himself two more horses somewhere, making three in all that he now owned. He would trade the lot for the "roan hoess." I tried to explain that the horse wasn't mine to trade. He belonged to another man, who was dead. Killed, by Utes, I added, and he nodded. But as far as he was concerned, if the owner was dead, then the horse belonged to whoever had him now, and that was me.

Maybe I would wrestle for him, he suggested. Red Leg liked to wrestle. Or gamble? He had a game involving two pebbles, held behind the back, and guessing which hand they were in.

I gave up trying to explain that it wasn't my horse, and just stated it flatly. No, I would not wager the roan horse. Not in any fashion.

He gave me a quizzical look, shrugged finally and turned away, back the way he had come, leading his two extra horses. Then as he came abreast the wall of rock he stopped, sat a moment in thought, then turned and rode back to us.

121

He would trade the two horses for a rifle, he said. He did not have a rifle.

I talked it over with Henry while the stolid Cheyenne sat his horse waiting for an answer. There could be no real harm in it, and we could handle seventeen horses as well as fifteen. I went into the cabin, got one of the extra rifles, and brought it out along with a large flask of powder and some ball and caps.

His eyes brightened when he saw what I was offering, but he took his time about it, making a critical appraisal of the rifle before he announced his decision. He would trade. Leaning forward from his perch he offered me the come-along on the two horses. Making very sure he understood what I was doing, I separated the straps and handed one back to him. I would take one horse for the rifle, and it was a fair trade.

"You ought to take the both," Henry said. "He took them from somebody else within the past few days."

What I had in mind, though, was to win a friend if I could.

Red Leg rode away leading one horse and carrying his new rifle. But as he left he again took a long look back at the corral and Henry said, "He hasn't given up on getting that roan."

The trade horse was a blaze-face sorrel, well-trained but peculiar-looking in the face. Its nostrils had been slit, the ways Indians sometimes do to increase a horse's wind. Out of curiosity I tossed a saddle on it. It didn't like it much but it took it, even trying to inflate its lungs when I reached for the cinch -- a trick no horse learns except by experience. Red Leg had no saddle. Most of the Cheyenne did not. This horse had come into his possession by very Indian means.

I was about to turn it into the corral when it dawned on me that it was shod. This was no Indian horse at all. A feeling like cold water spread across my shoulders.

"Henry, hold this animal."

I had seen no brand, but now I went around to the right flank and looked carefully, pulling back the winter fur. There, right where it should be, was a small brand that I knew well. Most of the horses in my herd carried it. It was the trail mark of all of Captain Mellett's herd. My face must have gone chalk white, because when I looked around at Henry his did, too—or as near as it could come. He couldn't see the mark from where he was, but he knew what I had found.

This was one of the animals taken by those who had wiped out the expedition.

"Ute," Henry breathed, and I just nodded.

The implication was clear.

"It's time to leave, Henry. Red Leg may have just brought your friends down on us."

"They are not my friends now, Randy," he said. I believe it was the first time he had ever used my name. "I have pulled my stick from the water."

Henry had ridden once with the Utes, and had not returned. They wouldn't welcome him again.

We spent the waning hours of the day, all of us, in frenzied activity. We filled packs, tied furs, mended tackle, and cleaned guns and tools. We would move out at first light.

Becky broke down and cried at the realization of leaving the cabin in the valley. I think that there in some mysterious way she had come back from a long and lonely journey.

But she packed and mended with the rest of us, and when nightfall came she was already making plans for the trip to Santa Fe.

I felt a sadness, too, at leaving. What had been a hole to hide in had somewhere along the line become a home to me, the best I could recall, all things considered. In a way I had taken root in these mountains and in this valley. I didn't really want to leave. With the possibility of Ute warriors on the way, however there was no choice.

It was a quiet supper we shared that night, the las in the cabin in the valley, and my thoughts turned again to the sad, senseless mystery of the man on the mountain. He had stood there above us, high on the altar of nature's great cathedral, and his voice had rung out in words of scripture to give conscience to the wild lands and the far places. I wished that we could have found him, could have helped him in some way. wished I could have known at least who he was. hoped he had died without pain.

When the fire burned low, I went out to check the horses and to look once again at the silver moonligh over the valley at the foot of the cathedral rock. For a moment, far off to the south, I thought I glimpsed fire light. Just a speck of it, and just for an instant. Then was gone. It might have been only a trick of the eye.

Henry came out of the cabin and stood with me fo a while, then wandered off toward the lower pond sniffing the air. When I looked again he was walking out beyond the foot of the great rock, dark in the moonlight, looking this way and that. And when next looked for him, he was standing two or three hundred yards away from me, out on the grass, mo tionless, barely visible. I watched him for a momen and something strange caught my attention. It was in his stance, his posture, his frozen attitude. With just a hint of something out of order I started that way.

The sky was clear and the moon was in first quarter casting a ghostly light. I was nearly to him before could see him in detail.

He was standing, frozen like a dog at the scent, hi rifle halfway up and his legs slightly bent at the knee As I came up he raised an arm and pointed, and looked to the north.

There, at the very edge of the valley entrance, along and above the lip of the cut in the shadow of the great altar stone, were fires. Six of them I counted. No, seven. Two were close enough that I could see distant figures moving around them. Campfires. How many men need that many campfires?

Henry finally looked at me, and I could see the glint of his eyes in the shadow of his face. "Utes," was all he said, then both of us lit out for the cabin at a dead run.

I don't think they knew we were there. The wind was from the southwest, what there was of it, but in that deep place the altar stone stood like a vane at the bend of the valley to carry smoke and smells upward, to swirl and eddy the air.

I think they had just arrived at the cut, following Red Leg's trail, as night fell, and decided to camp there and proceed in the morning. But I think they saw us when we saw them, and Henry thought so, too.

"Indians don't sit facing the fire," he said. "Only white men do that. Then when they try to look away, they are blind. We saw them; they saw us."

I had two Hawkens. Henry had the French rifle and his old musket, Mr. Sneed had his rifle, Jesse had the Kentucky, and we still had two of the outlaws' guns. I wished I still had the one I had traded off to Red Leg.

All the horses were secured in the corral.

We roused the others and checked all the firearms for load, brought all the packs and gear into the cabin, and cleared the middle of the room, piling everything around the walls. Mr. Sneed and I carried water until the rock basin in the corner was full, then knocked out chinks here and there in the walls to give a view in all directions.

After that the hard part of it began. The waiting. If they had not seen us out there, they would come with first light, riding through, and probably come for the horses when they discovered us. If they had seen us, there was no telling what they would do. They might come in the night or maybe with first light. They were a war party on the trail of horses stolen from them. They would not be friendly.

We slept at intervals through the cold, dark hours, Henry and I keeping watch by turns. Toward morning, a chill fog began settling, and by first light the valley was blanketed with a grey mist.

Visibility was good out to about a hundred yards, lessening beyond that to nothing. It was a ground fog, nothing more, but it was a hindrance. They could be almost in rifle shot before we would know they were there.

For an hour Henry had been fussing more and more. He paced from one wall to another, peered out, stood pondering, then paced again. As first light seeped through the fog, he made another tour of the walls, straining into the haze, his expression pensive. Then he stopped at the east wall and knelt, holding his rifle ready. "Now," he said. "I think they are coming now."

I set Mr. Sneed and Jesse at the west wall, facing toward the horse corral, then knelt beside Henry. Peering through a wide chink I could see nothing but the grey haze, with close features of the ground and the sandstone bluff just becoming visible. I had grown to trust the Indian's instincts, and I watched intently, seeking a movement, a color, anything out of the ordinary, as little by little the light began to build.

I saw him at the same moment Henry did, a lone savage crouched low, creeping along the very base of the bluff, not fifty yards away. His buckskin garb blended with the rock so that he was almost invisible. It was only when he moved that we saw him.

Both our rifles crept out through the chinks, and as they did he raised up and fired. I heard and felt the heavy ball thud into the log wall, close enough to my rifle to shower splinters in front of my eyes. Almost simultaneously Henry's rifle barked, and the Indian was jolted backward. He fell and didn't move again.

Becky was beside us and handed Henry a loaded gun, then set about reloading his with a detached efficiency I had not seen in her before. I glanced back quickly and saw that Mr. Sneed was holding his position at the west wall, not distracted by the shots. Jesse was nervous, but was staying with him.

I moved to the front, to a low port near the door. Almost immediately I saw movement there, out in the haze. But I couldn't make it out. Then it moved again, a warrior closing in, crawling, blending with the ground. He had a rifle before him and was bringing it to bear when I fired. It was a solid hit. He sprawled there, and in a moment I could see the blood. Becky was reloading the first Hawken, and I had the second one out and ready.

I don't know what I expected to happen then, but nothing did. There was a silence that went on and on. Little by little the light was improving, and I strained my eyes to see but could make out nothing extraordinary. The dead Indian lay there, a blur on the ground, barely visible except for the glint of rifle and the crimson of blood. I glanced away and then looked back but couldn't see him. My eyes weren't playing tricks. He was gone.

In a whisper I asked Henry if he could see the one he had shot. He could. I told him mine had disappeared and he shrugged. "Then he wasn't dead," he said.

After a while Becky asked me, "What is happening? What are they doing?"

I didn't know. Neither did Henry.

"The fog is bothering them," he said. "We can't see but neither can they. I don't know what they'll do next."

What they did came suddenly and almost worked.

One minute there was nothing, the next minute I heard Jesse's rifle fire and then there was a warrior coming at me, running, breaking out of that blanket of fog, and bringing his gun to his shoulder as he came. I fired as he did and saw my shot go home. His shattered a piece of chinking almost at my ear, burning me with the fragments. The sound was still echoing in the cabin when Henry fired, and I had barely brought the spare rifle up when a big, brawny brave burst from the fog and came in a weaving run. I fired as he bobbed. Then he was launching into a flat dive right to the base of the house, under my port. I had missed him cleanly, and as I drew the rifle in, the door crashed open, and he stood there, rifle at his shoulder, seeking a target. The first thing he saw was Becky.

He was squeezing the trigger when I hit him. I came up off the floor and drove upward into him, mashing him sideways against the door frame. The sound of his gun in the little cabin was deafening.

He was strong. When I hit him it should have broken some bones, but he was on me instantly, rough hands at my throat, pushing and crushing, his knee coming up. Over his shoulder I glimpsed another one coming in and heard the report of a rifle almost in my face.

His thumbs dug in. There was a ringing in my ears that shouldn't have been there, and my vision was clouded with a blood-red haze. I twisted violently, and his knee caught me on the leg. I drew back and thudded both fists, as hard as I could swing, into his midsection. It was like hitting rock, but the pressure on my throat lessened for a second, and I continued the motion, swinging both arms up, one fist clipping his cheek as they rose, and reaching high through his circling wrists. It broke his hold, and I brought my hands down again, one on each side of his head, chopping for whatever I could reach. My hands came together at the base of his neck, and I felt him flinch.

He tried a swing, awkwardly, and I hit his midsection again. I must have loosened something there before, because this time my fist sank in halfway to the wrist.

Then he stopped moving. He stood for a moment, his eyes going dull, a gout of dark blood spilled from his mouth and nose. He sagged and fell. With a twist I shoved him outward, then slammed the door and tried to replace the bolt. The wood hasp had been twisted and split. It was useless. As it closed I saw another Indian lying face down just outside, motionless.

It had all happened in seconds.

I got back to the front wall port, and Becky handed me a rifle. There was nothing out there to shoot at. After a moment Henry said, "How bad are you hurt?"

I wasn't, that I knew of. But there was something wrong with my arms. They felt numb. And as I noticed the numbness, it spread like a flame throughout me, and I just sagged there by the wall.

Becky came over, concerned and trying to help. There was blood on her hands when she lifted them.

It passed in a moment, the weakness, but my throat hurt like it was afire, and it was several minutes before it subsided. The Indian's thumbs had almost crushed my throat in that moment at the door. There was blood down my shirt where his nails had dug in.

When I managed to get back to the slit in the wall, there again was nothing to see. The light was stronger now, but the fog still held. Becky was reloading, and the rest of us helped, always keeping an eye to the outside where sunlit fog created a blind white world.

There was a dead Indian outside the west port, crumpled at the corner of the corral. There were two piled outside the door, one atop the other—Henry had fired across my shoulders to bring the second one down. And there was a buckskinned body by the sandstone cliff beyond Henry's wall.

Five were down, maybe six. We didn't know.

We were all unharmed, I thought, then it struck me that Mr. Sneed had not moved. I eased over beside him.

He had been kneeling, face and shoulder tight against the wall, looking out. The shot that killed him had come through a seam between stone and log. He had not even moved.

Jesse appeared at my shoulder, and froze, his eyes enormous. It was a second before he reacted at all, and then his eyes misted. He sagged against me, and his old long rifle fell with a thud against the wall. "Gramps . . ." he whispered. Becky must have turned at the sound, because I heard her gasp. Then she sort of choked and crawled across to where I knelt, my hand still on the old man's back. She was shaking, and I put an arm around her shoulders and held her tightly for a moment.

Henry stayed where he was, keeping an eye out, while I eased Mr. Sneed back into the corner and put a blanket over him. Except for the little bullet hole in his chest, he looked fitter than I had ever before seen him. His eyes were closed, and there was a hint of a smile on his face.

God forgive me, I wanted to pray but I couldn't remember how just then. What I did was sit there blinking to keep the burning out of my eyes while I whispered, "Mary, look after this old man. He's come

130

a long way to find you."

Something thudded against the log wall, and I turned quickly and took Jesse's thin shoulders in both hands. Just for a moment he continued staring at the blanketed figure that was his grandfather. Then he nodded, picked up his rifle, and went back to the wall.

There were no Indians in sight. With the guns loaded, including the rifle the brave had carried to the door, we waited for them to come again.

"They may wait a while now," Henry said. "You notice all these had rifles? They can't have that many rifles. Most have bows and lances. These were the first assault. They were supposed to get us. Now they'll pull back and think of something else."

I was thinking about ways to get the drop on them, maybe by going out there, and Henry read my mind. "You'd never get fifty feet," he said flatly. "They'll be waiting for some one to come out."

I did have one thought. "Henry, you remember what we told the Cheyenne about this place? About the spirit on the rock?"

He was thoughtful.

"Try it," I suggested.

"All right," he said, and looked around. His eyes went to the smoke hole in the roof. "There."

By dragging three of the loaded packs under the hole, we made a pile he could stand on and get his head above the roof.

"Can you see anything from there?"

"No," he said. "Nothing."

Then he started talking in Ute, not too loud but in a voice that would carry through the fog. He called the leader, Quanas, by name, then went on, the guttural language rolling forth into the fog.

He was still speaking when a rifle sounded out in the mist and a ball thumped into the peaked roof near him, showering bark and splinters down on us inside. Henry ducked so fast he fell off the pile of packs. Then he climbed back up and said something plainly derisive, then continued.

When he came down he was shaking his head. "I don't think they are impressed."

After a moment a voice sounded outside. It was a deep voice, chiding and abrupt, and spoke only a few words.

"He says I'm lying," Henry explained. "He says there are no spirits here but there will be soon."

"Then we just have to wait." We went back to our posts.

Chapter Fifteen

Finally, the fog began to lift and from the low chink-port where I crouched, I could clearly see the dead Indian sprawled out in front, half hidden in the grass. His rifle lay by his outstretched hand, and it gave me an idea.

There were four rifles out there, all within a few yards of the door. For the moment, no Utes were in sight.

I went out the door at a crouching run, scooped up the rifle of the Indian sprawled there and went right on past toward the one a little way off in the grass. I was almost there when I heard the twang of a bowstring and felt a searing pain high in my leg. Before I could turn my head I heard Jesse shout, and his rifle sounded. When I looked there was an Indian pitching forward on his face off to my right, at the corral. He must have been hiding there.

An arrow protruded from the side of my right leg, and I instinctively tried to pull it out. When I did, the rending pain seared through me, doubling me over. It took a half minute to recover enough for thought processes to return.

Then I took the shaft in both hands, as near the skin as I could grasp it, and broke it off. The shock of the

133

breaking wood almost curled me up again. But I could still move. With two rifles recovered, I scuttled back to the cabin door, pitched them inside, and went around to the south where I got the third rifle from the one by the bluff and brought it back.

When I appeared in the doorway Henry said, "Let's see your leg." and I said, "Not now," and headed for the corral. I got the other gun, a huge old flintlock with a bore like a hollow tree. The Indian lying there had a pouch on him full of heavy lead balls, and I grabbed them, too. We didn't have anything in the cabin to feed that monster musket.

I was rising to go back when Jesse yelled again and I turned. Three Utes were coming out of the haze, almost on top of me. Jesse's Kentucky barked and one of them suddenly had a third eye. The Hawken took another one out as he pulled his bow, and the third drove at me with a lance. I dodged and felt it graze knife-hot across my ribs, then smashed him down with the old musket, swinging it one-handed like a club. When he tried to get up, I hit him again, and he lay still.

I was dragging my right leg when I got back into the cabin.

"They were trying for the corral," I said, and Henry nodded.

For a time then all was quiet. I sprawled on the dirt floor, and Becky cut back the seam of my britches around the arrow stub, then called to Henry.

He came over, looked at the wound gravely and asked, "You partial to that leg, white-eyes?"

I was in no mood for Pawnee humor.

"Then lay still and don't holler," he ordered, and he drew his knife.

He fanned up the coals in the fire pit, heated the knife, and cut that arrowhead out of me like it was something he'd been after all his life. I don't remember much of what happened during the next few minutes, or the next hour. But pretty soon I was sitting propped up by the wall with my leg wrapped up tight in swathing, and things were finally coming back into focus again.

There hadn't been any action for a while, but the fog had lifted still more and was starting to break up in patches. Henry was fidgeting.

"I know Quanas," he said. "He'll try something else before his cover blows away."

They had reloaded all the rifles, including the ones I had brought in. We had quite an arsenal there. Henry was thinking now, quickly and with certainty. "Get all those guns out," he ordered. "You too, Becky. Mount them low and point them almost level with the ground. Group them here, and here, and two there and three over here."

He was setting up a broadside.

We waited for them, for the all-out rush that Henry was sure would come. "Whoever sees them first," he said, "just sing out and then we'll all fire, two at once each and then anything else that's poking out."

They did what he thought they would do. Becky saw them, yelled, and we all opened up in a full barrage. It sounded like the end of the world had come, and the whole cabin vibrated and rained dust and bark down on us. The Indians had been coming at us all-out. When those guns opened up, they just disappeared. I doubt if we hit many, if any, but it stopped the rush.

The minutes dragged by as we reloaded frantically, and for all the sound we could hear they might have been gone. But we knew better than that. They had a lot of reason to stay around. They wanted our horses, and they wanted our scalps. And they wanted the rifles they had lost — and ours too. But Quanas was cautious now. He had lost too many warriors.

The sun was beating down through the morning fog, high and brilliant. The moment came when we could see far out into the grass pasture, and what we saw was enough to take the starch out of us.

They were lined out there, spread in a wide circle across the pasture, twenty of them or more, just sitting their horses and watching. The fog rent into dying wisps, and golden sunlight played across their emblazoned buckskins and shone on the bright feathers in their hair and on the yellow and black paint daubed across their faces.

They were in no hurry. Maybe a few of them had rifles, but most of them had stout bows, and I knew what a driven arrow could do. They were in no hurry. They would wait until they were ready to move.

The long vigil at the chink in the wall had added a stiff neck to my other miseries, and I limped to the door, opened it and stood there in the sunlight stretching my muscles, leaning on the door frame. looked across at them, and they looked back. One of them drew a bow full back and launched an arrow high. It glinted in the sun as it came, arching downward, to thud into the ground not five feet from where I stood. I didn't flinch, didn't move at all, but I whistled low through my teeth. That was more than a hundred and fifty yards, and that arrow would have penetrated had it found a target.

Henry came up beside me. He pointed out a tall dark-skinned warrior mounted on a white horse. "Quanas," he said.

They were talking it over out there, some of them moving up and down the line now and then, and after a few minutes a couple of them rode over to the war chief and talked animatedly with him, pointing our way and gesturing. He studied us for a moment then said something to them. They wheeled their horses and galloped off down the valley to the west. One carried a rifle, one a bow and arrow.

We watched them as they headed for the gorge. They were going to get above us.

We were about played out. We might stand off another charge. We might even hold them off until nightfall, but they were going to win in the end.

But not without a fight.

"Henry," I said, "you and the kids will have to hold them off for a while. I am going to try to climb that bluff. I want to stop those two coming up the slope."

He looked me over a minute and shook his head. "You'll never make it, Ran-Da-Hay. You can barely walk. I'll go, if you'll distract their attention for me."

He was right. I didn't argue.

I stood there in the doorway while he slung two rifles on his back and refilled a powder flask. When he was ready, we walked out together, strolling toward the corral as though to look at the horses. The Indians didn't move. At the corner of the cabin Henry turned and leaned on the log wall, for all the world like he was passing a quiet Sunday in Independence town, and said, "If you have some idea about drawing their attention, go to it."

I had an idea.

I drew the big knife from my sheath, let its blade flash a few times in the sun, then strolled out into the grass and, with half the Ute nation looking on, began scalping dead Indians.

When they realized what I was doing, there was a buzz of loud talk and a lot of shuffling around in the line of redskins. One or two started my way, but I raised the Hawken, and Quanas shouted something at them. They turned back, shaking their fists at me. I went on about my bloody business.

It took four or five minutes to collect all those

scalps, and when I turned back to the cabin Henry was nowhere in sight. I took all the scalps to the front wall, waved them at the Utes and then hung them there by the door in plain sight.

An arrow thumped into the ground behind me somewhere as I finished tying up the trophies, and another thudded into the cabin wall a few feet from me. Out of sheer perversity, I ignored them and went back to the doorway to stand where I had been before, looking out at them. Just to top it off, I filled a pipe and lit up. I don't know how Henry went about it, but I don't think they ever noticed that one of us had gone.

If I had ever carried any notions about what fighting Indians would be like, I had abandoned them. I might have thought it would be a continual fight, a charge-and-run, fire and reload and fire again sequence, surrounded by the din of battle until finally one side or the other was victorious. It was nothing like that. The Utes were angry, but they took their time. They were in no hurry. Nearly an hour passed before the wide line of savages began moving again, and this time they divided into three groups, walking their horses forward in close-order march, each group fifty yards or more from the next. I watched, fascinated.

As they came, Quanas raised his lance above his head, held it upward for a moment, then swept it around to the right. Suddenly the squad to his right, to my left, was in full gallop, bows strung and Ute war cries rending the air. And oh, but they moved fast. Before I was aware what was happening they were thundering across almost in front of me, and as I dived back through the door two arrows sang above my falling back. I heard others thump into the wood beside the door. I swung around with the rifle, but they were already gone, circling out toward the open grass again. The second flank was passing them, coming in at a run.

Jesse fired but didn't hit anything, and as I slammed the door shut I heard that deadly rain of arrows on the wood again and felt the timbers quiver under my hand. Becky was at the far side port and fired one of the rifles there. As the pitch of yells outside diminished, a new set took their place, and the third platoon was on us. Two of them had rifles, and added their roar to the barrage.

Something was wrong, though. It was a frightening, fearsome display of savage cavalry in action, but it seemed senseless. They couldn't penetrate the cabin with arrows.

The first wave came across again, and I got in a shot at one, but missed, and pulled around to watch through the chink as they veered off again. There were five of them. There should have been six or seven, I thought.

I was rolling over and bringing the rifle up just as Becky screamed, and I shot the savage away from the smoke-hole in the roof before he could draw his bow. Another one took his place and put an arrow into the ground beside me before I could trade rifles. Then another appeared.

From the corner of my eye I saw a gun barrel thrust inward through a chink in the stone, a foot above the floor. Jesse saw it and jumped high to land on it with both feet. Outside there was a crack and a strangled yell. I shot through the smoke-hole again, missed the Indian there, but moved him back, and Becky said, "They're coming in, Randy!"

They were charging the door.

Far overhead somewhere I heard the crack of a rifle. Henry was up there, working, but it was too late. The Utes were all over the cabin, and even as I turned, the door burst open, and they were in, bows drawn, painted faces grinning in their victory.

My rifle was empty. There was nothing I could do. I heard another shot up on the mountainside. Then nothing.

It was strangely silent for a moment. Five or six Utes were in the cabin, arrows trained on us, waiting. Then Quanas stepped through the door. He looked us over, his eyes malevolent. Then he raised a long tomahawk and started for me.

What happened then was as though a legion of ghosts had descended upon the earth, and the earth became a strange and different world. From far above us, rolling out with thunderous power and a great depth of anger, came the voice of the man on the mountain, lashing down upon us, echoing out across the valley.

"Come near, ye nations, to hear: And hearken ye people . . ."

The Indians froze where they were. It was not a human voice but a voice dragged from the infinity of heaven or the depths of hell. It was a ragged, rasping voice, deep as from some unearthly throat, magnified, and echoing again and again among the mountain peaks.

"For the indignation of the Lord is upon all nations," it thundered. *"And His fury upon all their armies; He hath utterly destroyed them. He hath delivered them to the slaughter."*

Quanas ran out through the door to stand before the cabin, looking up. The others followed him, dragging us out with them. There were three Utes on the roof, a couple by the side walls, and a dozen sat their horses out in front. They were all motionless, their faces turned toward the top of the great cathedral rock.

Up there, at the very lip of the great stone, tiny in the distance, stood an outlandish figure wrapped in furs and tattered cloth, a bright Indian blanket thrown over its shoulders. The man was balanced on the edge of the precipice, his arms spread wide, his face upturned away from us.

"The slain also shall be cast out," he thundered, *"and their stink shall come out of their carcasses, and the mountains shall be melted with their blood!"*

The Indians around me stood stock-still, their dark eyes wide with surprise, all rooted where they stood by the unearthly spectacle, the unworldly thunder of that great voice. *"Inti!"* one rasped, and several others echoed the word.

As the buck beside me slackened his grip on my arm I pulled loose and backed off a step, but he didn't notice. Moving quickly I pried Becky and Jesse away from their captors, and we backed away toward the corral, forgotten for a moment as the rolling voice went on and on in magnificent anger: *". . . For it is the day of the Lord's vengeance, and the year of recompense . . ."*

Quanas looked away and shook his tall frame like a bear trying to rid itself of fleas. He was holding my Hawken in his dark hand and with swift motions he loaded it, and raised it to draw a bead on the roaring figure high above the rock. Becky tried to twist away from me, but I held her back. There was nothing we could do.

"It shall not be quenched night or day; the smoke thereof shall go up forever . . ."

Quanas fired.

The distant figure crumpled into a ball of fur and rags at the top of the cliff and seemed to hang there, at the very edge. Several of the Indians started to howl their delight, then went silent again as the figure on the rock straightened, rose full tall and for the first time looked down at us. I could not see his eyes from where we were. But I could feel them.

Two or three of the Indians gasped audibly, and several began to shake in superstitious terror. For a moment that dragged by there was no sound anywhere in that valley. Then the figure on the rock spread its arms out, hands toward us, and the voice we heard was a changed voice, more powerful than before, but deep and warm and charged with serene, unswerving love for all of us, white and red alike.

It was a voice to raise the hackles and to make the heart cry out, to chill the flesh and warm the marrow.

"The Lord is my shepherd," it said. *"I shall not want."* A brave standing near me dropped his bow from nerveless fingers.

"He maketh me to lie down in green pastures: he leadeth me beside the still waters. He restoreth my soul."

A moan went up from some of the Indians, and they began backing off, stumbling away from the rich sadness in the voice of the apparition above.

"Yea, though I walk through the valley of the shadow of death, I will fear no evil; for thou art with me; thy rod and thy staff they comfort me."

There was a thudding of hoofs and some of those beyond us on the grass turned tail and lit out down the valley at a dead run. Now the voice rose in pitch to a plea, a cry to powers beyond understanding as the ragged arms lifted again and the distant face turned upward toward heaven. *"Surely goodness and mercy shall follow me all the days of my life: and I will dwell in the house of the Lord forever."*

He didn't look down at us again. The world below him and all in it had ceased to exist with his final words. For a moment he stood poised there, then he seemed to cave in, to crumple. High and tiny, the figure wavered there at the lip atop the great rock. Then with a strength as vast as the mountain silences he straightened once more, spread his arms against the sky, and a sighing wind whispered through the valley.

Meadow grasses rippled and wept and the tops of conifers bent as though bowing before him, and I knew that was no man up there, at least no ordinary man.

Quanas shuddered visibly and his whisper was loud in the stillness that followed the wind. *"Inti."*

Han-Ra-Hay of the Pawnee had spoken of Deathwind. In his language Quanas of the Mountain Ute spoke the same.

When I looked up again the speaker of the rock was gone.

In silence they moved around us, picking up their weapons, bringing in their mounts, draping their dead across their horses. When they were done they filed past, their eyes straight ahead, going.

Quanas was up on his big white horse and as we reached the cabin door he cut in beside us, reached past as though we weren't there and took the Ute scalps from the wall, then leaned my Hawken there and turned away.

On impulse I called, "Quanas," and he turned back. I unhooked the dry scalp from my belt, held it out to him. "Uinay," I said.

He looked at me with haunted eyes. Then he took it and wrapped it with the others in a bundle behind the Spanish saddle he rode. Without word or sign he turned and galloped away after the file of Utes heading for the west gorge. We watched them until they disappeared around the final shoulder. Jesse sat in the doorway, his face white and drained. Becky leaned against the wall and began to cry. There was a rattle of stone behind the cabin and Han-Ra-Hay of the Pawnee came down carrying three rifles.

Chapter Sixteen

We buried old Mr. Sneed deep beneath a rockfall, and chipped out a rough cross on a stone slab atop it. Then while Becky and Jesse knelt there in the bright afternoon, I took Han-Ra-Hay aside and we looked upward toward the crest of the standing rock.

He had heard it from the mountainside, and now he turned to me and I saw the same ghosts in his eyes that were in mine. "Do you still think that was a man up there, white-eyes? I think you know better now."

And I could see it in the Indian way. That ragged body up there had been that of a man, but that great store of anger, of love and anguish, had been far more than human. The words had been English words, from the Bible, but that had been no human voice. He had spoken and the wind had answered. He had spread his arms and the world had bowed before him.

Deathwind had died up there. But Deathwind had lived.

"We should go up," I said.

"No."

"We should find out—"

"No. He will always be there. That is his place."

Maybe Henry was right. . . .

We left the valley early the next morning, pausing

only once — at the crest of the west gorge — to look back. We swung south along the base of the flanking ridge there, climbed up and over a long swell, and let the cathedral of the mountains slip from view behind us, hidden by the miles and the intervening crests.

I rode the roan, and Henry, his painted mountain horse. Jesse sat high on the buckskin, and Becky rode the Ute sorrel with the blaze face. Each of us led a pack animal or two, and we pushed the rest of the herd along. We stopped once during the day, in a pleasant little grove on a mountainside where a clear spring trickled from a crevice in the rock. We rested there a while and then went on.

By evening we had covered a dozen miles or more, winding an easy trail through the rugged mountain country. I was heading generally south. Somewhere ahead would be a wide, hilled valley where the main slope of the stony mountains cut back far to the west. And I knew that once over the pass ahead of it, we could angle southeast across that foothill land and must eventually cut the Santa Fe Trail, maybe somewhere near Bent's Fort.

With evening, the mountain air turned chill again, and we found a hollow place, back against an upthrust shale cliff, to make camp. My leg was stiff and painful, and my aching throat still produced rasping sounds when I spoke. But hot coffee, pemmican and bannock biscuits cooked on willow sticks eased the discomfort considerably, and when we rolled into our blankets I slept deeply and well.

Our campsite probably looked like a traders' rendezvous. I had all of Captain Mellett's spare horses, plus the buckskin, the sorrel, Henry's pony, and the big horse Uinay had ridden, Mr. Sneed's draft horse, and one horse from the outlaws. In addition there were four packs of furs, seven extra guns tied in a bale besides those we carried, about forty beaver traps, a quantity of tools and utensils, and a pack or two of staples.

The next morning we continued south under a warming mountain sun. An hour out Henry beckoned me to one side as we rode. He said, "I feel like we're being followed."

So we left the horses with Becky and Jesse in an aspen grove and scouted the backtrail for some distance, but found no sign of any sort. Henry shrugged, and we went back. He still looked worried, however.

That night as we buried the coals of our campfire in a hidden swale atop a low, pinon-clad mesa, I went out to look around before turning in. Again I thought I caught a glimpse of a campfire, just a spark on the dark shoulder of a peak some distance off, quickly lost to view. It was like the spark I had seen, or thought I had, on a mountainside south of us before the Utes had attacked. I slept lightly and woke often as the night hours passed, but nothing was amiss when dawn found us.

That day in mid-morning we descended into a wide, flat-bottomed valley ringed with rock and stunted pinon, where the spring grass grew deep and rich. A little stream wandered along the bottom land with narrow groves of cottonwood dotting its course. At its high end, the valley terminated abruptly at a sheered wall of red rock where weathered boulders lay half buried in the sod. The stream had its source here, springing from a cleft in the rock ledge to a pool among the boulders and then finding its way downward along the valley floor. We rested there, mending tack and letting the horses graze their fill on the high grass.

Henry saddled a disgruntled bay which hadn't been ridden lately, fought it down, and went off to scout out backtrail. I found a perch on a tall rock and settled down there to keep an eye out. The sun now had real warmth, and for an hour or so I alternated between guarding and dozing. Eventually Jesse came crawling up the slope, that long rifle sprouting from his small hand as usual, and said he'd take his turn at guard. There wasn't much guarding to do. It was a pleasant, peaceful place.

Down by the pond Becky was washing clothes, spreading the wet garments on rocks to dry. I started in to help, but she shooed me away. So I just sat for a while, enjoying the sun and watching her. When she pulled my old spare flannels out of the water and held them up, shaking her head in dismay at the havoc of knees and elbow, they were taller than her.

That girl washed everything we had loose except the various buckskin garb, and she would have washed those too if I hadn't objected. With some items of her own, she made me turn away while she scrubbed them.

When she had finished, she turned to me, soap in her hand, and said, "My turn now. Go away." So I did.

I was up on a rock shelf trying to mend some worn-out harness when she came up to sit with me, all fresh and pretty, and smelling of soap.

"It's so beautiful here," she mused, combing out her long golden hair to dry. "Can we stay here rest of the day, Randy? It's already past noon."

I had been thinking along the same lines.

"I suppose so. The horses could use a rest. And anyhow, it's Sunday."

She turned, skeptical. "How do you know it's Sunday?"

"I just think it's Sunday. It feels like Sunday, and chances are about one in seven that it is. So I hereby

147

declare this to be Sunday, the day of rest."

"Yes, sir," she said gravely. "And I can bring you your pipe and slippers, and you can read aloud from the scriptures, and we won't have dinner until four o'clock. Except," she said, looking at my beat-up old boots and giggled, "I don't think there are slippers that big."

It was good there, just leaning against a half-buried rock, feeling the warm sun soak in, watching a hawk hunt off in the distance, and now and then noticing the scent of fresh-scrubbed girl. The latter part was disconcerting.

"We should eat," she said. "I'll make a fire." But she made no move to leave, just sat there combing out her hair, her eyes closed, her face to the warming sun.

I took refuge in the thing that had become locked in my mind, the purpose I had accepted a season past when there was no other purpose to cling to. I had a responsibility. I must get those horses back to Captain Mellett's heirs. They were all that was left of a man I had admired. It was cold shelter, but it was better than letting my thoughts linger on the girl there beside me. Those thoughts, pleading as they were, simply had to wait.

A time passed, and she asked, "Randy, what's to become of us—of Jesse and me?"

I didn't know, but it struck me I had that responsibility, too. She and the boy, they had no place to go. When Mr. Sneed died, a responsibility had passed, and it had fallen to me.

"Oh, I suppose I'll marry," she said when I didn't answer. "Someone will take us in, somewhere, and a young man will come calling. He'll have his hair combed and starch in his collar, and he'll smell of bay rum." Her voice sounded a little bit strained, and she had turned away. Suddenly I felt I had hurt her some how. When I didn't answer, and should have, she had kind of pulled away.

There had been some right thing I should have said, and it was needed. But I couldn't bring it to mind.

"He'll ask me to marry him," she was saying, more to herself than to me. "And, of course, I will."

She got up, looked around again, and added, "My, but it is beautiful here." Then she went to build a fire. She left me there feeling like the world's prime ignoramus and wondering why.

Jesse eventually got tired of sitting on that rock up there, so I relieved him and found again that it was a dandy place to doze.

Henry was gone a long time. When he finally came in, the bay was tuckered out, and he had news.

He had scouted north, along our backtrail, combing several miles of country, but had found no sign of whoever had made the fire that I had seen in the dark of evening. "Has to be Indian," he said. "I would have found a white man's camp."

But later, circling back across the long ridge behind us, out to the west, he had found a body.

"White man, dead a couple of days. Four or five horses been along there moving south. I make it he was one of a group, and something happened to him. They stopped where he fell, then went on. Just left him laying there in the grass."

Varmints had been at the carcass, he said, and there wasn't much left to describe.

We tried to piece it together from what Henry had found—and he wasn't one to miss much. But there wasn't much to go by. A group of white men had passed to the west of us, going our way, maybe two days before. One of them had fallen. There were no signs of trouble, so whatever had happened to him had been further back. He had ridden until he fell, and the

149

rest had gone on their way. Their path and ours led in the same direction, but as far ahead as I could see, there was no place where the two trails would necessarily converge.

Henry wasn't impressed with my idea that today was Sunday, but he was amenable to putting another day between us and whoever had passed before us those few miles west.

That night Henry and I climbed to the top of the highest hill around. Up ahead of us, to the south, we saw nothing. But sure enough, back the way we had come, high on a slope, was that wink of firelight again, right where Henry had searched during the day. We hadn't moved today, and neither had the owner of that campfire.

By full dawn we were well down the valley, the herd strung out on leads so we could ride free. At length the valley veered to the right, then divided into two branch canyons. We selected the one nearest to true south, with Henry scouting out ahead.

We set a fast pace along the canyon floor, which opened out after a mile or so into a broad, deep valley seamed with gullies and hills. We threaded down a deadfall-tangled shoulder, then up a swale and onto a long ridge running south. Beyond it, with the sun going down, we strung along through a great open basin studded with rock and pinon stands, moving until last light.

In the grey of morning, we switched horses, repacked, and moved on. The terrain was changing around us. We were no longer in the high mountains. Rather we were just inside the flank of the east frontal range, that great wall of last defense before the foothills that spread away toward the endless plains to the east.

We made good time that day, letting the horses run

when they were willing and alternating saddle mounts twice. It was mostly open country, usually a mile or more between the ragged, shelving mountains off to our right and the rank of frontal peaks to our left. The snow was gone now from the flats, and green was everywhere. Only here and there, in a protected gully or behind a shaded north ridge, was there white to be seen — except high up on the peaks where crystal caps flashed in the sunlight.

That night we camped under the crest of a low swell where eroded spires made a last stand before giving way to the slopes of yet another broad valley. We ate a good meal and saw Becky and Jesse rolled in to sleep. Then the Indian and I climbed a point of rock from the top of which we could see for miles in all directions.

For a long time we stood there, seeing nothing except moon-bathed mountains around us. Then it was there, that same persistent spark of firelight that had dogged our trail for days. It was a bare, flickering spark of light up on a mountainside, above us and back the way we had come, but much closer now than it had been before.

Whoever was back there was following our trail, and closing in. We had moved fast for two days, and the pursuer was closer now than before. Han-Ra-Hay shook his head, as puzzled and troubled as I.

"All I'm sure of," he said, "is that's no white man out here. At least no kind of white man I've ever seen."

Henry took his blankets a little way back along the trail to spend the night there, and I took mine up in the rocks where I could see.

That speck of fire was still there when I went to sleep.

Chapter Seventeen

We moved early again the next day, long before dawn. We lined out at an angle down the slope and let the horses have their heads, clipping along through the early light at a mile-eating trot.

I was riding the roan and I let him have his way, taking the point position for a while. He fairly flew down the wide valley, and when I looked back the others were coming right along with me. I aimed for a distant point where mountain slopes on both sides pinched the valley down to a crack.

We were all getting spooky about the mysterious follower we had, and without discussing it we had just made up our minds to outrun him. Within an hour we were across the wide part of the valley and coming up on its outlet canyon. This was a high-walled fissure, a trench between the bases of two forested slopes, cut by time and water.

As we neared it, I called a halt, and Henry and I rode up the two swelling flanks of the canyon to look down from above. We saw nothing but canyon and came back down.

If ever there was an ideal place for ambush, I thought . . . and it crossed my mind we might wait here for whoever was behind us. But I didn't want a confrontation, not really. I just wanted away from that dogged fire in the night. We pushed on through.

Beyond, the country opened out. A long way off I could see rolling hills descending into the blue distance of midday, running out into miles where vision gave way to haze and where there were no mountains beyond. We had come to the great bend of the stony mountains, where the foothills thrust far west into the heart of the range.

It was a sight to behold, and I drew up to wait for the others.

As I did so, a shot rang out, and the roan horse pitched crazily beneath me, then collapsed. It hit the ground full length, a dead weight with my right leg mashed beneath its bulk. The Hawken spun from my fingers as my hand hit a rock. The roan's head came up, frantic, and it screamed, lurched frantically once and died. A red stain spread across its neck, just forward of the shoulder.

There was a dissipating puff of smoke up in the rocks at the side of the trail, and I saw a man crouched there, ramming a fresh load into his rifle. I rolled my shoulders around and stretched, trying to reach the Hawken. A ball cut ground inches from my face, erupting a gout of damp soil. I heard the sound of the shot at the same time, then the bark of another rifle off behind me. There were two more shots, then another, and suddenly our pack horses were thundering around me, headed down the valley toward the foothills. I managed to turn around on the ground, the pressure wrenching at my injured, trapped leg, a sick pain beginning to spread from it, and saw Henry and Jesse scuttling for the cover of a rock fall. Becky was sprawled at a shallow wash, not moving. Up in the rocks across the gully were three or four men. As I watched, I saw two of them raise and fire, and chips exploded from a rock just above Henry's head. He was down on his knees, ramming home a load. Beyond him Jesse raised and fired the Kentucky and the two men ducked for cover.

I couldn't reach the lost Hawken, but the second one was somewhere under the dead horse, its strap still secure on the saddlebow just over my leg. I tried to reach for it, and my fingers ground into the dirt, digging down. I felt the buttstock.

Another shot sounded. A ball plowed into the horse's body.

Suddenly I was fed up. I was so wracked with anger that my thinking processes ceased. I saw again the twisted mouth of the furious grizzly above me, and I saw the great fury of the roan horse driving into the bear, battering it to the ground—the same horse that lay dead atop my aching leg now. And in that instant I let human reasoning slip away. What replaced it must have been akin to the wild, unthinking rage of that horse when it lashed out at the bear. I pushed with all the power my shoulders could muster. Something cracked in my hand and a finger went numb, but I got hold of the Hawken and surged backward against it. It stuck, then slipped, and came free in my hand. Lying there on my back I raised my left leg, planted my boot on the saddle and lay the Hawken across my knee, raising my shoulder to come into line with the rocks up there.

There was a rock with a split base, and I knew there was a man behind it. I lay the sights on the top of the rock and squeezed the set trigger, then eased my finger on the firing trigger, took a deep breath, and waited. When he raised up I recognized my old acquaintance Hob Frierson from the creek camp. He turned his face toward me and I shot him full in the mouth.

Now I needed the other Hawken. With my boot still

154

on the saddle I gritted my teeth and lunged, shoving downward. The pain roared up through me and made my ears sing, but when I came to again my leg was free.

I rolled over, crawled a yard or so and had the gun. Henry's rifle sang out again from back in the rubble on this side of the wash, but there was no answering fire.

Becky was still down in the little gully, but she had moved around for better cover.

Then I saw another of them, a tall, bony man with red hair streaming from under a slouch hat. He had come down through the grass, stealthy as a wolf, and was crouched in a patch of nettles almost directly above Becky.

I was bringing the rifle around when she moved a little, and he saw her. He jumped to his feet, bringing the rifle down to fire, and the Hawken and two other rifles all roared together. The man simply came apart there at the edge of the gully, hit by three heavy rifles from two different sides.

I reloaded the Hawken I was holding, crouched there beside the dead roan. There would be two left. The big one, Felix Briole, and the thin Canadian, Mercer Cate. I swept the rocks across the way, then the valley above and below. There was no sign of them.

I tried to stand up. My leg crumpled, throwing me down again. "Henry," I called, "take a look in those rocks."

He came out of cover and ran, low and fast, across the gully and up the short slope. I covered from where I was. He disappeared into the rocks. After three or four minutes he came back. They were not there.

"Can you walk?" The Indian's eyes were on my swollen leg, which was bleeding again.

I tried, and again the leg failed me.

The horses were far down the valley, spread out and beginning to graze. "Better go get them," I told him. "Then we'll see about me."

Jesse had come to where Becky was crouched, and the two of them now came over to us. There was a smudge of dirt across Becky's face.

As they came closer she suddenly noticed the roan horse, sprawled dead there in the valley floor. She stopped and her hands went to her face, fingers at her mouth. "Oh," she gasped. Then, "Oh, God, no!" It ended in a wail.

To me, the senseless death of the roan had been a culmination of all the anger of months past. To her, I think it was a culmination of pain and terror and sadness. When she came to where I was sitting and knelt to look at my leg, big tears were streaming unashamedly down her pretty, dirt-smeared face.

After a second careful search of the rocks and the low cliff behind them produced no sign of either Felix Briole or Mercer Cate, Henry and Jesse set off down the valley to round up the horses. I lay back to endure whatever Becky had to do to fix my leg.

I was prepared for the worst, and it was a little disappointing when she said, "Oh, that's not so bad. Nothing's broken."

I lay back and closed my eyes.

I had lain there only a moment, letting the tension begin to drain from my keyed-up muscles, when Becky gasped and I opened my eyes to see her looking up, behind me, her face pale. When I started to turn a deep voice commanded, "Hold it right there, mister, and don't touch that rifle."

I turned around slowly, resting on one elbow. Felix Briole stood over me, huge and ugly, his bulk blocking out the sun. He had a rifle trained on my face.

156

He looked puzzled. "Who are you, mister? I've seen you."

I studied him but didn't answer.

His grip tightened on the rifle and he scowled. "Who are you?"

Becky had withdrawn to one side and was getting to her feet. Briole glanced at her and his eyes lit up. "Don't run off, missy," he said. "You and me'll talk later." Then he turned his gaze back on me. "I said, who are you?" he roared.

A chill came over me, and I felt something in that moment with a sure certainty. I was not ever likely to return Captain Mellett's horses to their owners. I was not going to leave these mountains. Becky had to get away from this brute of a man, and the only way was for me to distract him while she ran.

I answered him. "You should know me, Felix Briole. I shot at you and made you run."

"You shot—" he stopped. "You lie! That was some damn kid did that, and you're no kid, mister. You ain't him at all!"

"You're wrong, Felix Briole," I said. "Look closer."

He was not quick in the mind, that one. His reflexes acted before his reason did, and he leaned forward to peer more closely at my face. As he leaned, I lunged forward with both arms out, grabbing for his rifle barrel.

It went off in my face as my hands found it. The blast was blinding, the roar deafening and something exploded under my chest. "Run, Becky," I tried to shout. "Run and don't look back!" I clenched that rifle barrel and it snapped upward in my hands, then held.

My vision was blurred, my eyes stinging from the powder flash. My ears were roaring, and I felt the rifle sight cut into my hand as he tore it loose. I sprawled on my face, then pushed up on one elbow and raised

157

my head. Briole was standing above me, his legs spread, the rifle raised above him to strike downward. Suddenly he shuddered as though slapped by a great, invisible hand, and I heard the crack of a rifle. For a moment Briole swayed there looking totally, eternally surprised. Then he toppled backward and lay still.

I wiped a bloody hand across my face, trying to clear my eyes. Somewhere I heard Becky's scream, and a long way off someone shouted. When I looked up again a broad-shouldered, buckskinned figure was stepping down from a rock off to the right, pulling the ramrod from a rifle barrel. It was Red Leg, the Cheyenne.

He walked toward me and looked down, narrow dark eyes inscrutable. Then he moved on, to stand over the body of the roan. For a minute or more he just stood there, head bowed, looking down at the dead animal.

"Roan hoess," he said finally, to no one in particular. Then he straightened, strode past me and pulled a knife from his belt. He stooped by the body of Felix Briole and his eyes shone with a devilish light. "Roan hoess," he repeated. As I watched he began cutting fingers off the fallen outlaw.

When he was done he looked back once, mostly at the dead roan, then shrugged his shoulders and trotted away over a rise, heading north.

I heard voices somewhere behind me, and running feet. Then I didn't hear anything.

Chapter Eighteen

They rounded up all the horses that had scattered out across the flat. Then they scouted around and found the outlaws horses picketed in a draw not far away where Briole's bunch had waited for us to come up. There were pack animals there, too, and packs of furs someone had gathered during the winter months.

Between them, Henry and young Jesse collected the lot, and with Becky's help they moved everything down into a wide rock canyon with a good grass bottom and made camp there. They found a running spring back a ways and carried water from it. They put up a lean-to against the base of an overhang and spread a good bed under it. The bed was for me.

They did it by themselves. I was no help at all. I woke up once to find my right leg and my chest bound up thick in tree moss and clean sacking and a blurry sort of Becky fussing over me with cloth and a pan of hot water. When I tried to shift position, the pain in my leg made me howl. When I reached for the place that hurt, I couldn't feel it because of the bandages on my hand. And when she said something to me I couldn't hear a word she said. On top of it all, my face was on fire. Being awake right then was a waste of time, so I quit.

Sometime later it was night, and the stars over the far wall of the canyon looked hazy and blurred. Jesse was sitting slouched on a rock near me, a rifle across his lap, his little body relaxed in sleep, his face drawn in the flickering firelight.

Then it was morning again, a pink, gauzy morning with field larks singing their hearts out for the sheer joy of it and Becky doing good things to my face with cool water. And then it all ran together. Outlaws and painted Indians charged up and down over my head, shooting at me, pointing at Captain Mellett's horses, and the roan was falling, and falling, then the sweet face of a golden-haired girl kept coming past, looking to me for help, needing more than I could give but needing it all the same. Two tender faces: a little boy with haunted eyes and tight-lipped courage and a girl with the look of a woman about her, both hiding behind me when the outlaws and the painted Indians came again.

After a while it faded, the tension eased and I knew mountains, brilliant in the lemon light of morning, shining in the high-noon hour, regal above cool forests of scented pine where fat deer paraded along a babbling stream. It was beautiful, and I wanted to stay, but I had to sink away below it, away from it, back to . . .

To the spectacle of a cynical savage with a dead bear's face on his head, offering me a cup of hot coffee and saying, "Well, it's about time you woke up."

I tried to come up with a choice insult, but all I could get past my throat was a dry rattle. So I took the coffee, raised my head with his help, and drank a little of it.

"Henry," I managed after a few tries, "you'll never know how close you come to looking like hell."

"Your appreciation touches my savage heart," he

said. "Drink your coffee."

I wanted to get up and about, but it didn't seem worth the effort just then. I was lying on a soft pallet under a roof of cottonwood boughs, at the base of an overhang shelf. The sun was shining, the air warm and fresh.

The Indian came back after a while, refilled the coffee cup, and then sat down cross-legged beside me and lit a pipe.

"I've been taking inventory," he said. "All told, we have twenty-seven horses, eighteen rifles, nine packs of furs, about sixty dollars in gold coin that your white friends don't need anymore, and various other salable items. Not bad for a known fool and a heathen, Ran-Da-Hay."

He was right, in more ways than one.

"No sign of the fourth man?"

"Sign enough. He slipped away from them. Lit out south. He's gone."

"What's been the matter with me, Henry?"

He puffed on the pipe and the cynical expression left his face for just a moment then resettled itself there.

"Nothing much, really. It was the arrow in your leg that did you in. It must have festered, and then when you got that leg mashed like that, well, you just took sick in a hurry. Aside from that and a rifle-ball crease along your wishbone, along with a cut just above the short ribs, powder burns on your nose, a broken finger and a cut-up hand, an ankle that's swelled up like a snake after dinner and several sprains and bruises, you are in excellent shape.

"There's really nothing much wrong with you," he added, "except you're beat all to hell."

I decided I didn't feel like getting up after all. But a little later when Becky came around with a pan of thick buffalo stew cooked up with greens and wild roots, I put it all away and called for more.

We stayed at that canyon for eight or ten days, and when we left I was astride Billy's black horse, leading the herd out, heading south.

Chapter Nineteen

From the plateau country we angled south-south-east, guided by the sun. We traveled across a land of hills and pinon stands, high grass and antelope, with buffalo herds coming north to meet us. This was the home of the Arapaho, horse hunters and fierce hunters, akin to the Cheyenne of the eastern slopes, but through the days we spent traversing the region we saw Indians only once.

As we topped a rise coming down into the basin of the Arkansas River Jesse spotted movement ahead of us, and we circled up the horses to wait. It was a whole tribe on the move, coming down out of the mountains toward the Great Plains to the east. We were nearly a mile to the side of them when they passed, and though they saw us—several braves rode toward us for a distance and sat facing us until the rest of the tribe was well past—they showed no more than cautious interest in us.

It looked to be eighty or ninety people in all, with their women and children, and their worldly goods packed on travoises. They moved in a spread-out line that stretched a quarter-mile along the greening valley. When they were finally out of sight, we moved fast, straight down into the broad basin and then into the flats fronting the river.

It was late evening when we crossed the river. We let
the horses drink and rest for a while, then used leads
to take them, a few at a time, on up the south slope to
a gentle valley a mile or so beyond the stream. We
camped there and stood careful guard, but the Arapaho did not return.

I had hoped to make Bent's Fort, but we missed it
somehow — too far west, I reckoned — and headed
south into the western rim of the Purgatoire breaks. It
is hard to imagine that there can be any more magnificent desolation anywhere on earth than these wide,
torn plains above the headwaters of the Cimarron.
Buffalo were here in abundance, and antelope, and
here and there we saw great wild cattle with horns
longer than a man's arm. And through the long, sun-
baked days of travel there we found no sign of anyone

On a warm afternoon when the sun was sinking toward great massed cloud banks on the distant peaks
we came down into a flat shortgrass prairie. There
were tracks of numerous wagon wheels, spread wide
across the plain, curving west and south into the distance. We had found the Santa Fe Trail.

We camped a night at a place where a cold spring
seeped from the rock of a great plateau and pooled at a
grove of cottonwoods in a hollow, barely visible from
the main trail. Then another night we spread our roll
atop a high, grassy knoll in treeless country where the
land lay limitless on every side and the stars above us
were twice as bright and twice as many as they nor-
mally appeared. And finally on the fifth day on the
trace, we saw in the distance the purple slopes of the
Sangre de Christo Mountains, beyond which lay
Santa Fe.

The main freight yard in Santa Fe was a bustling
place, and it cost me four dollars to arrange storage fo

the packs and furs and tending for the horses. When we rode into town it was the first civilization I had seen since leaving Independence a year before.

It wasn't much of a town, old and Spanish, and all bunched up together, but it was bursting with life. All up and down the main street there were people coming and going, a motley montage of humanity milling busily around like ants on a bothered hill.

It takes a little conscious thought, coming down out of the mountains like we were, to adjust to having people all around you like that and most of them not after your scalp at first sight. We seemed to make no impression by our garb, and indeed there was a variety of costume around us that might have addled a gentle person arriving here unaware. There were Spanish Mexicans with great sombreros and fringes on their pants, American teamsters and buffalo hunters, here and there an hidalgo in stiff finery, and a great many somber Indians. There were few ladies in sight: a couple of matrons window-shopping in front of a store, corsetted in the style they were calling Victorian after the English queen, and a spring wagon with a sunshade and splash panels rolled by with a Spanish lady sitting aloof on the padded seat between two wicked-looking vaqueros.

Becky, though, with her yellow-gold braids hanging long down the back of her short doeskin dress, slim leggings tight across shapely knees as she straddled the buckskin, drew some admiring glances. There were a couple of loafers in front of a cantina who appeared ready to crack some comment as we passed, but then they looked a little closer at Henry, and at me, and held their tongues.

There was a building two stories high partway down the new American street with a sign that said Regency Hotel. We drew rein there at the hitch-rail and went in. The man at the desk had to throw his head back to see us through his spectacles, and looked as though he doubted whether he had any rooms to let. But Henry grinned in that way of his and allowed as how he did, and the man decided Henry was right. The fellow brightened considerably when I laid out gold money on the board.

Henry and Jesse and I got a room upstairs, and Becky had the one across the hall from it. After we stowed our gear, we met down in the lobby and went shopping.

For a town short on size, Santa Fe was a cosmopolitan place in what its merchants could display. There was one many-paned glass window with nothing but ladies' hats in it and another packed with apothecary concoctions, penny candy, cigars, and tins of tobacco, and all sorts of stays and whalebone harness. At another shop the whole window had only a man's suit in it — black frock coat, strapped breeches, dove-grey vest and cravat, and a tall beaver hat. Henry was enthralled. He stopped at that window, and when I looked back from down the street, he was still there.

The general merchandise store didn't have a window in front, but it had big double doors open wide, and there was a well-stocked look about the place. We went in there.

I picked out some breeches and shirts for Jesse with ease. Then I started fumbling through the counter of women's things and sort of ground to a halt.

There was a pleasant-faced lady there who came to my rescue. She turned out to be the proprietor's wife. When I told her I wanted some nice things for Becky, she looked her over, held out a hand to her and said, "How do you do? I'm Mrs. Brown."

And Becky answered right back, poised and pretty as you please, "And I'm Rebecca Frost. It's a pleasure

166

o meet you, Mrs. Brown."

"I take it your husband is having difficulty choosing or you. May I help?"

I know Becky turned red, and I think I did. At any rate Mrs. Brown glanced back and forth at us and said, "Oh, I am sorry, I misunderstood."

"That's all right," I told her. "But I'm just caring for her and her brother until we can find them a place to go. They're orphans. Indians killed off their people up north."

Mrs. Brown thought it over, gave Becky a sympathetic look, and took charge. "You go away," she said. "We will attend to Miss Frost's needs."

I went to look at boots and clothes, and outfitted myself with what I needed. I got Jesse some boots and a hat, too, and when I got back to the counter Mrs. Brown and Becky were wrapping up a great bundle of things.

I paid for all of the things we had bought—Becky's packages came to twice as much as Jesse's and mine together—then we went back to the hotel. There were washrooms there in the back, but I decided I wanted to go to a barber shop. I left Jesse and Becky at the hotel with the understanding that we would meet back here about sundown and have supper in the dining room.

There was a tonsorial parlor on the nearest side street where I got my hair and whiskers trimmed and my ears dug out. I paid out a coin and headed for the bathhouse. Clean and dressed in new town clothes, I felt almost civilized again. But I didn't look the same anymore. The barber had a mirror by his chair, and when I first looked in it I didn't recognize my own face for a minute. It wasn't just the beard or the powder-burn scar across my nose. It was something else. The last time I had looked into a mirror, a year or more ago, I had seen an overgrown boy looking back at me. This time I saw a man who had been to the Shining Mountains.

After that I walked around a while, breaking in my boots and looking in windows. There was one place that had a long rack of guns inside on the wall, and I went in and looked them over. There were mostly percussion rifles there, a few flintlocks, and several gleaming new rifles of the Paterson type designed by Colonel Colt, the kind that holds its charges in a rotating cylinder and will fire them as fast as a man can cock.

The gunsmith was waiting for me to decide to buy something, but what I asked him was, "Do you buy rifles?"

He said he did and glanced at my Hawken, but I told him it wasn't this one I wanted to sell. When he asked how many, I did some rapid calculations and said, "Thirteen."

It didn't bother him at all. He wanted to see them, so I went and got the whole bale except the second Hawken, Jesse's Kentucky, and Henry's French rifle, which he had with him, and carted them back.

We made a deal. I got one of those Patersons and a fair amount of difference, although seeing what he would sell them for, the gunsmith did all right, too. But it more than made up for what we had all spent at the general store, and when I walked out there I was carrying both a Hawken and a Colt Paterson. One to shoot straight and one to shoot a lot. I would decide later which I preferred.

When I got back to the hotel a man waiting there by the desk looked up and said, "Mr. Kerry." I said I was, and he stuck out a big square hand. "Fitz O'Brien's the name, sir. I run the freight office where you left your packs and animals." He was a short man, bandy legged, but barrel chested and thick in the shoulders.

168

He had a cheerful, businesslike way about him. He inclined his head toward the barroom next door. "I'd be obliged if we could talk," he said.

He waited while I went upstairs to leave off the Paterson rifle. Then we went into the bar and sat at a table, toward the back. He ordered beers—'cervesa' he called them—and got right down to business. I had furs and he was buying furs. Would I take thirty dollars a pack for them?

"Of course not," I said, and he grinned. "Then let's talk business," he said.

He started at thirty-five and I started at sixty, and we were homing in on forty-five and fifty when there was a commotion up front, where several men stood at the bar. I looked up to see Henry coming in. But it was not the Henry I had seen before. I recognized the bearskin cape and the French rifle, but very little else.

The bear-head hood was thrown back to make way for a grey beaver top hat, and the cape was open wide at the shoulders to show off a black frock coat, strapped breeches over black boots, a dove-grey vest, and a cravat tied under a frilled collar. He was smoking a long, black cigar.

There was absolute silence in the place as he strode up to the bar, elegant and cool, and demanded a beer.

"I'll be damned," O'Brien breathed, and I said, "That's my partner, Henry."

"Henry?"

"He's an Indian. I found him up in the mountains."

O'Brien nodded, still enthralled at the vision of gentlemanly attire standing up there at the bar. "Looks Pawnee," he said.

"He is. His name's Han-Ra-Hay. It means Mountain Cat."

He looked puzzled. "That's a Ute name," he pointed out.

I nodded. "He thinks he's a Ute," I explained, and O'Brien gave up and bid forty-five dollars a pack for the furs. I suggested forty-seven. We agreed, and he called for more beers.

As we visited I asked him about the Murphy brothers, who should have been around here somewhere. He thought for a moment, then looked around and spotted and old fellow in buckskins, a hard-looking old man, sitting alone at the back wall.

O'Brien raised his voice, "Mr. Underwood, would you join us?"

The old-timer looked us over and then came across and sat down.

"Mr. Underwood," O'Brien said, "this is Randall Kerry. He was asking about some Murphy brothers; one's name is Tad."

The old trapper, for that was what I took him to be, gave me a long, careful appraisal before he asked, "Would his name have been Thaddeus?"

"Yes, sir, it is."

"And why might you be wanting to know about the man?"

"He is a friend of mine, sir. We were in the same expedition, with his brother William and others. Tad left me and some friends to go find his brother. That's the last I've heard of him. I gather he is here."

"He never came here," Underwood said. "Your friend is dead. I know naught of his brother."

He was quiet for a while, then he hitched his chair in closer to the table, leaned on his elbows, and told me the rest of it.

Less than a month ago, Mr. Underwood had been with a party up in the Sangres. They had met and talked with a mesa tribe coming up from the winter grounds below Ten-Mile Peak. The Indians had found the body of a white man and had taken a locket from the body. It was Tad Murphy.

"I don't believe Injuns killed him," he said. "I know those mesa people, and I trust what they saw. I make it your friend ran afoul of brigands up in those hills. He was robbed and knocked in the head. By the Eternal, there's a few around would do it."

So that was the fate of Tad Murphy. I would miss him, I knew.

Anyhow, I wound up telling them the whole story. Tad and the children, Mr. Sneed, the winter camp, and finally about the outlaws up by the great bend. They listened intently, not missing a detail. When I got to the names of the renegades I knew, O'Brien's eyes widened and Underwood scowled, his eyes yellow as a hawk's under lowering white brows.

"Frierson!" O'Brien exclaimed. "And Briole too? Sir, you must live on the side of the angels."

"Damned good riddance!" was Underwood's only comment. Then he asked, "And who was it, if ye know, that ran away?"

"I believe I know him, from descriptions I've had. It was a Canadian, name of Mercer Cate. I've seen him. I once shot a powder horn off his hip last fall when the same bunch tried to steal my horses."

Underwood and O'Brien exchanged a glance, then O'Brien told me, "Mercer Cate is here in town, Mr. Kerry. I'd watch for him if I were you."

"He wouldn't know me," I said. "He never saw me there, or my partner either, that I know of."

Underwood was pensive. "I regret Mr. Murphy's death, I surely do," he said. "He was a good man, from what you say of him."

"Do you suppose it could have been the same bunch?"

"Could have been," Underwood answered. "But we likely won't ever know."

While we were talking another ruckus had developed over at the bar, this time building up slowly in raised voices and then erupting all at once. I had noticed in passing that a couple of teamsters standing there had seemed overly interested in Henry even after the novelty of him had worn off for everyone else. Now a chiding voice was raised, "Damn Injun acts like he was people."

I glanced up, and O'Brien and Underwood looked around, just in time to see Henry methodically poleax a teamster with his rifle butt, then begin shedding his finery and folding it carefully atop the bar. The second one, a man a head taller than Henry and fifty pounds heavier, was plainly astonished.

"You damn Injun, you brained ol' Abner!" he shouted. Henry was folding the bearskin cape, laying it on the bar. Then he started shucking off the frock coat, ignoring the man.

"You're gonna pay for that, redskin!" The teamster started toward him, but Henry held up a hand imperiously. "Just a moment," he said, folding his coat. "I'm not ready yet!"

"Not ready!" The teamster was aghast. Then he launched into a head-down, bull-like rush, and Henry stepped aside and planted a knee in his ribs as he passed. "I said I'm not ready yet," he said, and took off his top hat, setting it on the pile of garments on the bar.

The teamster was just getting his feet squared away under him again when Henry added cravat and vest to the stack and turned around, dropping into a lithe crouch. "Now I am ready," he said, and suddenly he was in the air, cat-quick, to plant his feet in the teamster's chest, bowling him over backward.

The teamster was strong. He hit the floor and rolled, and as Henry backed off, he caught him with a swing that almost brought the Indian down.

"A dollar on Sanderson!" someone called from the door.

As the bigger man came up off the floor, Henry dropped and rolled into the man's legs, upsetting him again, this time on his face.

Before the teamster could get up the Indian was on top of him, drawing one arm up behind the man's back, raining blows on his ears and the back of his skull.

"Five dollars says the Injun!" someone offered.

Two or three other men — packers or swampers they looked to be — seemed about to join the fray, and I was getting to my feet when O'Brien roared, "You boys just stand quiet! Let 'em alone!" They relaxed.

The burly teamster was struggling to his feet, Henry and all, and the place was filling with men attracted to the entertainment. The teamster shook himself like a bull buffalo, and Henry was thrown off his back. He landed on his feet and started in again as the big man turned and drew back a great fist.

Suddenly the fight was over. A rifle butt speared out of the crowd and caught Henry behind the ear, and he crumpled to the floor. The teamster looked around, puzzled.

I was on my feet and pressing through the throng when two men stepped forward and stood over Henry's limp form. I knew them both. One stood lopsided, favoring a useless right arm hanging from a crippled shoulder. The other was the Canadian, Mercer Cate.

The cripple was babbling, "That's him, Mercer, sure enough. That's the Injun that was with the kid that shot me. That's the one that sat there tellin' Hob what all he could make of a white man's skin, while I laid there bleedin' like to die.

"Kill him, Mercer. Open his skull up for him. Go

ahead!"

The big teamster, Sanderson, turned on them.

"Now hold on . . ." he started, but Cate's rifle was trained on him, and there was murder in the man's dark eyes. The teamster backed off.

Cate looked around the crowd. "Is the kid here, Clay? The one that messed you up?"

I was moving forward, and Clay's eyes locked on me as I pressed through the crowd, but passed on to other faces. "Reckon not," he said. Cate looked appraisingly at Henry, lying still there at his feet, then shifted his grip on his rifle and raised, muzzle up. I shoved the last two or three bystanders aside and put the Hawken an inch from his face, pulling the set trigger.

"If you so much as wiggle," I said, "you are a dead man. Now let that rifle fall beside you."

He did as he was told, his dark eyes scrutinizing me.

I asked him quietly, "Does your leg still bother you, Cate, from that busted powder flask?" Clay gasped and backed off. "Mercer," he rasped, "I think that's the one."

"You know it is, Clay," I said with ice on my tongue.

Then as they stood there, I let all the cold anger of the mountains rise into my throat and turned it loose upon them.

"Clay," I said, "I want you to walk out that door right now, and keep right on going. Don't ever get within rifle-shot of me or my friends again." He hesitated, his eyes wide, and I growled, "I mean right now, Clay! I left you one good arm. I'll leave you nothing next time."

He turned abruptly, mechanically, and the crowd parted for him. I didn't watch him go. All my attention was on Mercer Cate.

The man's eyes were unreadable, cold as a dead

174

fish, flat, and cruel. "I've never seen you before, mister," he said. "I don't know what you're talking about."

I shoved the hair-triggered rifle forward, and he stumbled back a step, losing his composure.

"You know exactly what I'm talking about, Mercer Cate," I told him. "I know you for a horse thief, a pack-robber and a murderer, and I suspect much more. Do you deny it?"

He was regaining his balance. He said coolly, "Of course I deny it, sir. You are a madman!"

"It is witnessed, Cate. Four men heard Tad Murphy accuse you before he died." No one had heard any such thing, but it worked. The veneer slipped away and his eyes flashed at me. "The man was a fool!" he snapped. "Traveling alone, he deserved to be robbed."

"And so you knocked him on the head."

"And if I did, who's to make me answer for it? You? You won't shoot me standing here. You had your chance before and you have it now, but you won't kill me. You are a fool, sir. Now stand off from me."

I gripped that rifle, and I wished him dead. My finger was hovering at the hair trigger. But he was right. I wouldn't shoot him. And when he saw me realize it, he turned slowly, picked up his rifle, and walked out the front door. I let the hammer down easy on the Hawken.

Fitz O'Brien, standing at my side, shook his head and said, "You should have killed him, Randall, while you had the chance. He won't give you a chance next time."

Old Underwood was at my other shoulder, a good Pennsylvania rifle in his hand. When I caught his eye, he nodded. "Pleased to meet you, Mr. Kerry." And he eased through the remaining crowd toward the door.

Henry was trying to sit up, a hand to his head, and the teamster he had clouted with the rifle stock was coming around. With the help of O'Brien I got Henry to his feet, and then Sanderson picked up his friend. We took them both outside to clear their heads.

Sanderson gestured toward the Indian. "Good man," he said. "Rassles like a redskin, but good."

Henry had a glorious knot on his head, but nothing else was substantially wrong. When I got him back to the hotel room, he flopped on a bedstead, and groaned for a while, then decided he wasn't going to get any sympathy, so he went to sleep.

I retrieved his rifle, coat, cape, hat, and cravat, returned them to the room, and went downstairs. I told the fellow at the desk that my friend desired to be awakened at sunset, and that his taking care of this would assure his being in the Indian's good graces for another day. Then I went walking some more.

I had noticed a few soldiers around town earlier in the day. There was a stockade of adobe brick out beyond the edge of town. It, like the town, had a substantial look to it as though their builders were determined that this bit of civilized ground in the middle of the wilderness would hereinafter remain civilized.

The Mexican War had produced very little effect in Santa Fe. One day General Kearny rode into town with troops and declared the place United States territory. No one argued at all. The alcalde welcomed him, the American traders in town shrugged, the Spanish landowners ignored him, and the little town continued its hum of commerce. The only difference had been the raising of the Stars and Stripes each morning instead of the colors of Mexico and the founding of an English language newspaper.

It was a pleasant, carefree little town, and I found myself wishing I could stay a while. But I had a task yet to do, and that was to close the account on Captain

Mellett's furring brigade by delivering what I could of his property to whomever was entitled to it now.

I was back at the hotel when the sun went down and went to find a table in the dining room. There were a few people already there, and eventually the room began to fill up. When Henry arrived, sore and irritable with a bump on his head, a pretty young lady with a white apron served us coffee.

Eventually Jesse came in from the lobby, spotted us, and came to join us. For a moment I did not recognize the blond young woman with him. Her hair was done up high on her head, and the dark blue dress she wore matched her eyes and molded her figure to the waist, above a full skirt sweeping to the floor. She was followed by Mrs. Brown. I almost knocked the table over getting to my feet, and when I tried to think of something to say, nothing came out.

As we held the ladies' chairs for them Henry said, "Becky, you've changed."

She was looking at me when she answered him, "Thank you, Han-Ra-Hay. I surely hope I have."

I had recovered my composure then enough to say, "You look very nice, Becky," and she smiled for me.

I am sure whatever we had for supper was good, because Henry ate his helping and called for seconds. Later, over coffee, Mrs. Brown asked what our plans were for the future. Henry just shrugged and the others looked at me, so I explained it. I had goods to deliver back East, and must return there. Also, I thought I would try to make arrangements somewhere for Becky and her brother, where they could get by and where Jesse could get schooling.

"They have no kin, you see . . ." I was explaining, when Mrs. Brown nodded.

"Yes, I know that, Rebecca and I had a long chat this afternoon. Tell me, Mr. Kerry," she asked, "do you

177

have a place in mind?"

I was saying that I really didn't, yet, when her husband came into the dining room, and she turned to wave to him. He joined us, a stocky, pleasant-faced man of middle years with bushy brown sideburns and an ink smudge on his nose. His wife introduced us, and he sat down, slumped for a moment and expelled a long, satisfied sigh. "Thought I'd never get it shut down tonight, honey," he told his wife. "I reckon half the people in town just remembered something they had forgotten to get all day. Martha!" He signaled the waitress. "Just coffee for me, please!"

The Browns were nice people. Ordinary, everyday people enjoying life in the best way they knew how, by keeping a general store.

After a while Brown's eyes lit on Henry, speculatively, and he said, "That's a fine suit of clothes, young man, but with your coloring you should have a red vest. Stop by the store in the morning. I may have just what you need."

Henry brightened considerably.

When we parted Mrs. Brown told Becky, "I do hope you will come around tomorrow, dear, so we can talk some more. I'll put a pot on and we can have tea and watch Clarence work."

"I'd love to," Becky said.

Upstairs we talked for a while in the little parlor at the end of the hall before going to our rooms. I told Becky and Jesse about the deal I had made with O'Brien for the furs, and that a full share was theirs. Becky's eyes moistened and Jesse's grew large. He whistled. "That's two hundred and thirty-five dollars," he said, and I nodded.

"Now," I said, "there are some good schools in Independence, and I'll take you there if you want to go, or we can go on to St. Louis, or even Chicago if you like

Wherever you two decide, I will see you there and established."

They looked at each other, then at me, then at Henry, but neither said a word.

"You think it over," I said. "There's no hurry. We will stay here a few more days until I can find a freight crew or a stage going east, and then Independence will be our first point of call."

I saw Becky to her room; then Henry, Jesse, and I went to ours. I lay awake for a while listening to the town sounds below the window and the singing of coyotes off in the distance. Later I dreamed of vast high mountains singing in the lonesome wind.

Chapter Twenty

Breakfast was slab bacon cut in thick strips and fried, with flapjacks, syrup, and black coffee. The four of us ate together. Afterwards I left them, got the black from the livery, and headed out to the freight yard. O'Brien wasn't there when I arrived, but he came in soon after, and we talked about the horses. I didn't want to sell them, I told him. They weren't really mine to sell.

I told him about Captain Mellett's expedition and how I had made up my mind to return the horses to his heirs, and he said, "It's a good thought, Randy, but it isn't practical. Horses are worth a good bit out here, but not so much back East unless they're thorough-breds. Tell you the truth, they aren't worth driving all that way, even if you fellers could do it, which I doubt.

"For a fact, all them heirs could reasonably expect is a return off whatever furs the expedition took — probably half the total. The horses, and other equipment that's all outfitting. Usually stays with the trappers."

I shook my head impatiently. "But I'm all the expedition there was left to trap, Mr. O'Brien, and I only got a short four packs. That's just a hundred eighty eight dollars. The horses are worth several hundred dollars, even back East, and if the captain left famil

180

behind, they may need the money."

He looked at me shrewdly, one eyebrow drawn down. "You've learned a lot about the wild country in one short season, Randy, but I don't think you know much about business yet." Then he shrugged. "All right, this is what we'll do. I'll post the herd here for you, and give you a letter of consignment. That means you can sell the horses or transfer them just by selling or transferring the letter. So whoever holds the letter will own the horses. Then the owner can either claim the herd or write me to sell them on commission or sell the letter itself back East. It'll be a bearer note."

I thought about it and nodded. It made good sense.

Then we got around to my travel plans. O'Brien had a freight string making up for Independence right now, leaving tomorrow. After a little persuading, he was agreeable to having the four of us travel along. Henry and I would double as guards and scouts, and do some of the hunting along the way to free up a couple of his men to help with the wagons. Before I left, we settled for the nine packs of furs, and I rode back to town with a fortune at my belt.

At noon I found Henry, down at the gunshop admiring the wares, and we went to the hotel for dinner. While we were waiting for the fried steak and greens, I counted out the money on the tabletop and separated out the four packs' worth for my catch. I put back half of it for the Mellett heirs. That left ninety-four dollars, and I shoved half of it across to the Indian. "This is our share for the winter, redskin. Forty-seven dollars apiece. Not too bad, considering."

He started to balk, then changed his mind and took it. "I guess we both earned it," he said.

I had enough on top of that, from the guns and gold, to take care of the hotel bills, incidentals, and travel.

After dinner Henry took his money back to the gun-shop and bought himself a new Colt six-shot revolving handgun. It was a handsome thing.

We were in front of a harness shop when Becky called to us from across the street. She was standing by the door of Brown's general store, looking pretty as a picture in her new dress. When we crossed over she said, "I must talk with you both," and led us inside.

Jesse was there, up on a ladder helping Mr. Brown stock some shelves. Mrs. Brown was over by the food staples straightening jars and things around. She looked nervous, and her husband glanced around quickly as we came in, then went back to what he was doing. We went to the back where there were some chairs and a table and sat down.

Becky gave us each a long, searching look and then clasped her hands in her lap and looked at them. "Randy," she said, "Han-Ra-Hay . . ." For a moment she paused, then looked up and said, "We have decided what we want to do. Jesse and I, I mean. We want to stay here, and Mr. and Mrs. Brown want us to stay."

I guess we didn't know what to say, so we just stared. She looked at us, pleading for us to approve. Then it all came out in a rush, "Oh, Randy, it is such a pretty town, and the people here are nice, and the weather is so pretty. There is a good school, too, an American school, where Jesse can study. Mr. and Mrs. Brown have no children, and they want us to live with them. And I could help in the store, and earn regular wages, and . . ."

As she ran out of words I heard a sound behind me. The Browns and Jesse were standing there, sort of huddled together like children doubting whether Christmas would really come.

Henry nodded. "I vote with them, Randy. I think

t's just what they should do."

There was no way I could argue it.

That evening the six of us had dinner together at the hotel, and we tried to think of all the things we should tell each other that it would be too late to say tomorrow. I knew I would think of a hundred things later which should have been said that night, but they just didn't come right then. In general, all I could think about was that it seemed too soon, too abrupt. I wasn't ready to lose her yet. I hadn't really had a chance to find her. And I thought how it was going to be, from then on, not seeing Becky's bright eyes around anymore.

It was as though she was reading my mind. She put her little hand on mine and said, "Come back, Randy. We wish you would—I hope you will."

"With starch in my collar?" I asked finally. "And my hair all combed, and smelling of bay rum?"

Her eye brightened, then started to fill with bright moisture.

"Yes, Randy. Oh, yes."

That night we moved their belongings to the Brown's house and put the buckskin and the sorrel and their gear in the Brown's barn. And I gave the pouch of fur money to Becky and Jesse—the entire full share.

When we started to leave, Jesse shook hands with both of us, then turned away abruptly. Becky pulled Henry's face down and kissed him. Then she turned to me and reached up, and when I leaned, her arms went round my neck and her face was buried in my shoulder so that I could barely hear her whisper, "I will wait for you."

Before dawn the next morning, we were packed and out at the freight yard, adding our bit to the bustle of a wagon train getting ready to roll. It was a big train, seventeen wagons in all, each with a driver, and a swamper riding brake, plus two trail scouts and four guards and hunters. Henry and I were two of these.

The trail boss was a man named Shelby, who rode a dun and carried a Colt rifle. He spoke in a voice that could be heard a mile away upwind. Roy Sanderson and Abner Hays were there, each with a wagon to drive. Sanderson gave us a friendly wave when we rode in. I thought at first that Hays was going to jump Henry, but they stood there comparing the knots on each other's heads for a minute, then grinned and shook hands.

As the sun topped the saddleback pass to the east, Shelby galloped forward to the head of the line, raised his rifle, and pointed it toward the light.

"Shake 'em loose!" he roared, and whips cracked at the head of the line, drag chains rattled, and harness creaked, and the wagons began moving one by one.

"Spread 'em long!" the bull voice commanded, and the lead driver loosed a stream of profanity and laid his whip out above the team's ears. As he pulled ahead, the second did the same, then the third, and so on.

When the whole train was moving, stringing out along the rising road, Shelby cast a hard eye over the line, then turned to canter ahead. "Move 'em out!" he sang, and the song of the wagons gained a rolling rhythm as they moved.

The Browns, Becky, and Jesse had driven out in a buckboard to see us off, and when Henry and I turned on a far rise to look back, we could see them still there, tiny in the distance, watching us go. We had to run our horses, finally, to catch up to the receding train.

No more than two hours out we came to the ridge where a high saddle contour thrust out from the mountains which fenced the Santa Fe slopes on the north and east. The wagons speared up the long fan toward the pass. Henry and I were riding lead, front-flanking the head wagon, just sight-seeing as we went. Suddenly I saw movement on a rock shoulder ahead and back to one side of the road. Calling Henry and another rider up, I spurred forward to have a look before the wagons came closer. It had been just a suggestion of movement, a reflection of something bright. I thought I might be wasting my time, but I wanted to be sure.

Caution learned in the high mountains has a way of staying with you. The trail wound left and down out of sight at the crest, around an outcrop that looked like the bow end of a keelboat. The shoulder was just beyond, back to the left of the trail on a rugged wash-cut slope which angled off toward a distant peak. When we came around that outcrop we had our rifles up and our eyes open.

Two rifle shots sounded, almost together. A ball went singing over my head so close I could feel its backwash, and as the black tensed, I brought the Hawken up toward the sound.

A man appeared on top of a rock, and I laid my sights on him. Yet, somehow, he didn't look just right. He was facing around to one side, and he stood in a peculiar, off-balance way, hunched forward. He turned slowly toward us, and I recognized him. It was Mercer Cate, looking at us, past us. As I started to squeeze the trigger he seemed to sag, then his legs buckled. He folded in the middle, dropped his rifle, and pitched headfirst off that rock to land inert at the base of it.

Someone was scrambling down the slope across from us, and when we came up to Cate's body, the old trapper, Josiah Underwood, came into view across the road. He was ramming a fresh load into his long gun.

He came over and looked down at Cate with us. "I

almost shot too late," he explained. "This'n had a bead on one of you."

Henry was studying the old man, his eyes level. "You've been trailing him," he said, not a question but a simple statement.

"Reckon so. Didn't cotton to him hardly a'tall."

We angled to the left of the rising sun, heading always north-northeast, out across the arid breaks of the Kiowa lands.

It being spring, and water holes reliable, Shelby took us by the Cimarron route, straight out through the wild lands and into the high plains, across the shortgrass country. Now and again we saw antelope, always going away. Nearly every day there were buffalo. Once the train was stranded for most of a nervous day by a huge herd of the shaggy brutes that came grazing indifferently past us. They came by the tens of thousands, migrating slowly north in their seasonal cycle, filling the air with dust and the hot stench of their massed bodies. For the time it took that herd to pass we waited, crouched and cautious around the wagons, lighting no fires, talking only in low voices, and making no sharp sounds. If that herd should decide to run, they would all go the same way. And no matter what the direction, they would leave nothing untrampled where they went.

We hit the Arkansas eventually at the trail's upper crossing, and a band of Kiowa watched us cross. From there we turned due east, following for a day or so along the river's north bank, into the great flint hills region. On a hot summer afternoon we pulled up south of the big natural fort of Pawnee Rock. There we made an early camp and spent an extra day resting the stock and mending tackle.

The further into the tall grass plains we rode, the more Indians we saw, but these were mostly friendly. On one occasion, Henry and I were riding out ahead of the train when a group of five Indians in buckskin breeches and homespun shirts crested a hill before us. After a moment's pause Henry spurred forward to meet them, and when he came back he said, "Pawnee. Smoke Hill tribe, my mother's people. We're getting close to home, Ran-Da-Hay."

In the second week of August, with the great bend of the Arkansas far behind us and the Kansas River paralleling our track to the north, we came into settled lands. Tilled fields lay here and there on the best land of the bottoms. Now and then we could see a house, and once a spring wagon passed us on the road with wide-eyed children hanging out the back, waving at our drivers.

Along the way, we saw several Indian villages nestled among the low, rolling hills, flanked by farms and small cattle herds. When we came to a campsite, we had hardly unharnessed the teams before several farm boys descended upon us and hung around long enough to wangle a meal and then sit back, wide-eyed and listen to the outrageous lies the older drivers told them about the wild and woolly West. I imagined, watching them, that those boys looked very much like I had looked not much more than a year ago. And some of them, like me, would sooner or later take the trail toward the Shining Mountains.

When one of them edged his way over to me and said, "What's it really like out there, mister?" I told him the truth. "It's worth seeing, son. It is truly worth seeing."

One thing I noted, as I had several times on the trip, was that Henry was in thick with Sanderson and Abner Hays, particularly Sanderson. They got along very well, and now and then in the evening I would see them walking off somewhere, their heads together, talking in low voices. It reminded me of the way I had seen Henry and Fitz O'Brien talking the evening before we left Santa Fe. I had been alone in the hotel room, finishing my packing and stowing the oilskin wrap with the bearer letter for the horses in my saddle pack, and had gone down to the street for a stretch and a smoke before turning in. They had been outside the hotel, deep in conference, and had ceased the conversation abruptly when I joined them. It had aroused my curiosity at the time, but I had forgotten about it later.

Well, maybe Henry had a deal going. The Pawnee was a slick one when it came to dealing, and I wished him well. He was a good man, for an Indian.

I hoped if he did have something going he would let me in on it. I was nearing the end of my mission that I had set for myself back in the mountains, to deliver Captain Mellett's goods to his heirs. I had clung to that when there was nothing else to cling to, and it had become firm. I would not rest until the Mellett expedition was as completed as I could complete it. It was an obsession.

Yet I was more and more aware that, when that was done, I had no plan. I had notions of working for a stake somehow, making a new start, building a life of substance, and the notions were all tied in with going back to Becky. Not with nothing, but with something to offer her.

I wasn't planning yet, though; I was just winding down the great adventure that had come to nothing for so many good men out there. It needed to be complete so it would be ended.

Maybe Henry was planning; maybe he had a trail for us to follow from then on. I hoped so. Somewhere back there I had begun thinking of Henry as my partner, and the thought was a comfortable one.

The next campsite was deeper into the settled lands, on a bluff overlooking a little flat-bedded stream where elms grew thick in the bottom lands and hardwood trees clustered on the quiet hillsides.

We angled then toward the Kansas River and met it where it ran into the muddy Missouri. At the fork, across the river, was a great city of Indian lodges, hundreds of them of several kinds. There were hogans and wigwams, sturdy sod huts and a good collection of brightly painted tipis. Several tribes had come together here in the summer season for a powwow, as Sanderson called it. Henry slanted a cross glance at him. "These people don't powwow," he corrected. "These are Plains tribes and river people—Dakotas, Pawnee, Wichita, maybe some Kiowa. They're here to trade. It's a *trading*."

As we moved on, toward a little settlement topping the next rise, Henry looked back several times.

Evening shadows preceded us into the village of Westport on the Missouri. As we pulled up at the edge of town the word went back through the train. "One more day to Independence, boys! One more day and home!"

As campfires sprung up and kettles clanked among the bustle and clatter of unharnessing the teams, I rubbed down the lineback I had been riding some of late and turned him out with the remuda.

Henry was already in and unsaddled, and I saw him across the way deep in conversation with Sanderson. It came to me then that Henry was planning to go back with the next train west. Well, fine! The Indian would make them a good hand, and he seemed to enjoy the travel, the work, and the freedom of a freight-line train.

If that was the case, though, I clung to the thought, maybe he was thinking about both of us doing that. Maybe he had us both in mind. He surely hadn't said anything about it, but maybe that was where our partnership would take us next.

Still, I had no rein on him. Henry might have some ideas of his own, and that was all right, too, if that was how it fell.

As I was eating meat and beans at a campfire a little later, watching evening's glow spread across deep Kansas sky, Sanderson wandered over, pulled up a keg and joined me.

"You and that Indian been through a lot together," he said.

"A good bit, I guess."

"You've got a real friend there, you know."

"I guess so." I waited for whatever he was getting at.

"What I mean is, if a man should ever go to judge a friend, it's a good idea to start with the fact he is a friend, if you follow me."

"I haven't the least notion what you're talking about, Roy."

He thought about it a minute. "Thing is, sometimes different folks have to go different ways and it's a shame if anybody makes wrong of that when it happens. And that's a damn good thing to keep in mind, even if it don't seem right at the time."

Sanderson never was a wealth of information.

It was some time later, when I was about ready to roll in, that I turned at the sounds of hooves and then sat up. Henry was there, mounted on his own paint pony, saddle pack tied on behind him. He wore buckskins and his bearskin robe. He nudged the horse forward and leaned far down to extend a hand to me.

"I'm getting off here, Randall Kerry," he said. "I wish you happy hunting."

I got to my feet, looked at him for a moment, the savage who had been my friend through the mountain time, and I was not as surprised as I might have been. I was going my way. He was going his. I took his hand.

"And good hunting to you, Han-Ra-Hay. I will miss you."

His eyes widened. "You knew I was going?"

I nodded. "I guess I did. I just don't know why . . . why here and now?"

Unreadable black eyes rested on me for a moment, then shifted away. "Because it's time for me to go," he said. He kneed the pony and turned away, then looked back. "That is the first time you have ever said my name."

He put heels to the paint. "Happy hunting, Randall Kerry, old Ran-Da-Hay!"

The night swallowed him. Just like that, Han-Ra-Hay was gone.

Chapter Twenty-one

Independence was a bigger town than Santa Fe, but with an entirely different feel. Where Santa Fe was like an excited youngster, reveling in its pure exuberance, Independence sat back stone-faced and disapproved.

Such a comparison wouldn't have occurred to me during the years I had lived there with my uncle. I had just cleaned up and changed into town clothes, and was slogging across a mud street toward the freight agent's office, when it struck me. The difference between the East and West was the walls. In the West, walls were used to keep enemies out. In the East they were to keep neighbors out.

The freight agent remembered Mellett's expedition all right, "the madman setting out on Pike's route" and asked what became of him.

"He died," I told him.

Records of the outfitting showed Mellett to be from St. Louis, and somewhere in the ledger the man came across a letter from a St. Louis firm, Johnson & Breck, inquiring as to the whereabouts of Captain Mellett. The letter was dated only a few months ago, signed by a Mr. Breck.

"Creditors, apparently," the man told me, and could

tell me nothing more.

It would be St. Louis, then. But first I had an errand of duty.

My uncle's house was as I remembered it, sitting far back on a weedy lot. I tied the black at the porch rail and knocked on the door. It was a disappointment, seeing him then. For one thing, he was smaller than I recalled, and where I remembered him as cold and stern, my impression now was of a bitter, humorless little man inclined to conniving.

He received me with the civility called for, and we talked for a while. Only once did his interest perk up and that was when I mentioned the money from the furs and the paper on the horses. I saw the interest and hastened to add that these were committed assets, not my own.

I won't go into that visit, except to say that when I left his house again, I left for good. A year and more ago I had walked away from there, travel-itchy and desperate. Now I rode away disenchanted. The pressures that had bred my first departure, so serious to me then, were insignificant in retrospect. When I left him this time, however, there was no breaking of bonds. Those had been broken long ago.

I arranged to run lines on a barge for passage down river for me and the black horse. When I went aboard I found Sanderson and Abner Hays already there.

"We're goin' to New Orleans," Sanderson explained. "Gonna have us some fun, then pick up a load and get it back up here for the spring run to Santa Fe. Want to come along?"

I thanked them but declined. Since leaving Santa Fe, I had a feeling that the great world had closed in around me a bit, and the feeling had gotten worse as we drew nearer to civilization. It was a lot of things half forgotten, the smell of cities, the gauntness of the dray animals hauling along the muddy streets, the angry voices always to be heard, the speculation and suspicion in every face — in short the general flavor of the East.

When I talked to Sanderson and Hays about it, one evening on the river, I expected them to scoff, but they both nodded. "It's a fact," Sanderson said. "Course you only see a little bit of it out here. If you really want a taste of civilization at its worst, try Philadelphia. Or New York. A man gets shut in like a cat in a box trap, and there's just no way to get out."

That didn't sound reasonable, at least not about Philadelphia. Becky and Jesse had come from there, and I pointed that out.

"Yeah," the big teamster said, "those young'uns have the open spaces in their souls all right, just like you and me. But it's like you said. They're *from* there."

We talked a little about Henry along the way. "There was a time there," I told them, "when I figured you fellows and that Indian had a deal going of some kind. I figured he would either stick with me, or with you boys and O'Brien. Surprised me when he left."

Sanderson looked away. "You just never know about Indians," he said, and changed the subject.

When I got off at St. Louis they got off too. To see the sights, they said.

And there were some sights to see. The town cloaked itself in casual elegance and sat there on the riverbank counting its money.

I left the teamsters at a waterfront place and headed uptown to find the office of Johnson & Breck. "Let us know how you make out!" Sanderson called. "We'll be around here someplace."

I was a rarity in St. Louis, carrying a rifle. Most men here bore pistols or swords, or both, and some carried no discernible weapon, although I always had the feeling that there was one there somewhere. But aside from the rifle, I blended right in. I had repacked my buckskins and was wearing town clothes.

Johnson & Breck, Investments, was located in a dingy little second-floor office right downtown. When I went in, there was a cross-looking clerk writing figures in a ledger book and a closed door behind him.

"My name is Randall Kerry . . ." I started, and he glanced up.

"Sit down, sir." He gestured imperiously toward a straight-back chair in the corner. "I'll be finished here shortly."

"I am looking for Mr. Breck," I persisted. "It's about Captain Mellett."

He looked up again and squinted at me. "You will have to wait a few minutes, sir, until I finish here."

So I waited, I guess twenty minutes. The door behind the clerk opened once and an angry-looking man stamped through the outer office and slammed the hall door behind him. The clerk reached around and closed the door to the inner sanctum again.

Eventually he got around to me. "May I have your name, sir?"

I had already told him once, but I told him again.

"I want to see Mr. Breck," I said, and he frowned.

"Mr. Breck is a gentleman of some importance, sir, and very busy. Please state your business."

I was getting more than a little irritated. "My business," I said, getting up and standing over him, "is with Mr. Breck. It concerns a furring brigade —"

He shook his head. "This firm no longer does business with trapping enterprises," he said, and started to open the ledger again. He couldn't, though. My hand was on top of it.

I leaned close and spoke distinctly, in case he hadn't understood the first time. "I am here to talk to Mr.

195

Breck."

He let me in to talk to Mr. Breck.

The latter was a close-eyed man with muttonchop whiskers and a bald head. He looked extremely irritated that I was there.

"Very well, sir," he said. "State your business."

"My name is Kerry, Mr. Breck. Randall Kerry. I was with Captain Mellett."

He frowned and held up a hand. "You may save your wind, Mr. Kerry. I have already heard of that investment's untimely end, and I assure you, you have nothing to gain by coming here." When he gestured absentmindedly toward the door and started to turn back to his papers, it was the final straw. I rapped my rifle stock on his desk.

"I have come here to speak with you, sir," I told him slowly, "and you are going to do me the honor of listening." He was listening. "Now first, do you know if Captain Mellett had kin?"

"Kin?" His eyes were blank.

"Family, damn it! Relatives. Anyone."

The close-set eyes were still startled, but a shrewdness came into them now.

"The captain had no kindred heirs, Mr. Kerry. But he did leave an heir. It is this firm. Have you something to report?"

It was a disappointment. But I had come this far. "Yes, sir, I do. I was the only survivor of the expedition, but I did some trapping."

The shrewd excitement faded. One man cannot trap that much. He said, "Of course the proceeds are due this firm."

I was already pulling out the pouch containing one half the payment for my four packs. I tossed it in front of him. "I was paid for four packs of furs, at forty-seven dollars the pack. That equals one hundred and eighty-eight dollars, Mr. Breck. This is your half, as creditor to Captain Mellett."

I suppose I expected him to say thanks, but instead he came out of his chair with his face turning purple. "Ninety-four dollars!" He almost choked. "My principals lose their investment in an entire expedition, and you bring me ninety-four dollars?"

I thought he was going to either spit in my eye or have a seizure at that point, but he placed his chubby palms flat on the desk top and lowered his voice.

"Understand this, sir," he rasped. "Captain Mellett was a fool, and he gulled my predecessor into going along with him. Then to top it off he got himself killed before showing us a return on investment. And now you—you come in here with this ridiculous trifle trying to win my favor or whatever you are trying to do—"

He was losing control again. "Out!" He pointed to the door. "Get out, sir, and do not come back or I will have the law on you."

When I left I slammed the door hard enough to rattle that clerk's teeth. As I stamped down the stairs I was fuming. I had crossed half the mountains and the entire Great Plains to deliver goods to Captain Mellett's survivors—and the only heir apparent was an imperious little tyrant in a dingy office who ordered me out. All that, to deliver money and horses.

The horses! In the anger of the moment I had forgotten the horses.

I dug into my coat for the oilskin package and pulled it out. Might as well make it complete.

The bearer note wasn't there. Fitz O'Brien's letter of consignment was gone and in its place was a crude note on a piece of paper wrap.

It said, simply:

"I hoped you would come to your senses, but you

did not.

"I told you once you are a fool, white-eyes. I was right.

"I also told you that I would take your horses.

"Best regards. Your friend, Han-Ra-Hay."

The Indian had done it after all.

It was two or three hours later, and evening was drawing on when I found Sanderson and Hays. Rather, they found me. I was at one end of a plank bar in a rough waterfront tavern, a good number of drinks of bad whiskey under my belt, and four river-rats were at the other end of the bar considering the value of my boots and rifle. I was getting impatient, waiting for them to make up their minds whether to jump me. I was ready to start the ball right then. I had a notion I could demonstrate the value of my rifle and my boots to their satisfaction.

Sanderson and Hays wandered in and dragged me out before the demonstration really got started.

"Don't never walk into a place like that alone!" Sanderson instructed me when we were a good way down the street. "It's a better way than Injuns to get yourself killed."

"However," Hays suggested, "It's all right to go into places like that with friends."

We did. Several of them. Later, by the grace of God, we found our way to a hotel to sleep it off.

We hung around town for two or three days, seeing the sights, and they wanted me to go on to New Orleans with them. But I didn't really have the heart for it.

The evening before left we had a long talk, and Sanderson worked himself up to making a speech. It sounded like it had been rehearsed.

"I told you once, Randy, how it is with friends. If one of them does something the other doesn't like, the

198

other one needs to take his time about finding fault. There may have been more to it than meets the eye."

"Is that what you said?"

"That's what I meant to say. What I'm saying now is, don't hold it too much against Henry; that Pawnee done what he thought needed doing. Take my word for it, Randy, you have a friend there."

"Had a friend," I corrected him, a little sadly. "But don't worry, Roy, I don't hold it against him. Those weren't my horses to begin with. And the way things worked out I'm glad he has them. I have no hard feelings."

When they asked me what I planned to do, I admitted I didn't know. Get a job somewhere, I supposed. Get a stake, then see what kind of future civilization offered.

"You ain't cut out for that, Randy," Sanderson said. "Why, man, the world's full of folks like me and Abner that can do the jobs. You ought to look in a mirror sometime, man. It's writ across your face plain as day. You've seen the Shining Mountains, Randy, and you ain't ever going to fit no place else."

"You mean go back?" I had thought about it. "Now?"

"And what else?" The big teamster's face was dead serious.

Hays nodded. "Go back, Randy. There's nothin' here for you anymore."

"But for what?"

"Why, man," Sanderson said, his arm waving away the little tavern around us to paint vast expanses of God's earth in its place, "for anything. For being there! That's what them mountains is for. You recollect times on the trail, you telling us about your valley up there in the high country? About that big rock there and all?"

I did.

"Go back there, Randy. The way you talked about it, I could see it. I could smell the pines and hear the high winds singin' overhead. Why, those mountains are in your blood. That's where you'll find your fortune. Don't fight it. It's your place on earth."

I thought about it, after they had gone. And I didn't fight it. Two days later I packed my gear, got new shoes on the black horse, slung my Hawken on one side of the saddlebow and the Colt Paterson on the other side, and headed upriver toward Independence.

Chapter Twenty-two

It being late in the year, there were no trains making up for Santa Fe and west, but there was other movement. There was a steamer going upriver to the Dakota lands on the high Missouri, and a late wagon train heading west and north to pick up the trail of the Mormons who were gathered around Bridger's post, they said.

"Damn fools," a tall young Irishman labeled them. "Winter will catch them in the high Plains sure, and they'll never see the mountains. Wagons and oxen don't move fast."

His name was Will Shannon, and he and a group of four were heading out on their own to try their hand at prospecting in the Sangre de Cristos.

There was also a mail stage for Santa Fe—the first of its kind and quite an occasion—but there was no room for passengers, and no chance of a man or a party on horseback setting the same pace. The stage would travel too fast if all the fresh teams were ready along the line, too slow if they weren't.

When Will Shannon and his crew left Westport, I rode with them.

The mail stage caught us at Pawnee Rock, and while we shared a camp for a night, I wrote letters to

Becky and to Fitz O'Brien and got them aboard. I wished them well and said I hoped I would see them in the spring. Watching the stage depart with those letters, I realized how much I wanted that. A feeling of loneliness had settled upon me. Part of me longed for a valley below a standing rock in the Shining Mountains. Another part held close the image of a Viking princess in doeskin garb. More and more as the months went by, I had realized the little girl with the newfound laughter was very important to me.

At the great bend of the Arkansas, we angled a little north into the open lands and then straight west. We held that course through bright days and chilly nights.

We encountered Indians once. We came across a small herd of buffalo straggling southward through the shortgrass hills. Will and another of the team, Barney McDowell, wanted buffalo coats like mine, and all of us were wishing for fresh meat, so we rode down on the flanks of the herd to pick out a couple of fat animals. As we came down-slope, angling in from behind the herd, Will drew rein and pointed across the wide draw. Four mounted Indians were angling toward the same herd from the other side, all carrying rifles.

"Arapaho," I said, and we pulled up where we were, rifles out and ready. The Indians had seen us too, and they drew up facing us, three hundred yards away. For a moment we just sat there, each party waiting for the other to move, and then one of the braves on the far slope held up a hand and brought it down slowly, sweeping down toward the buffalo.

"I think he means we are invited," I told them, and I repeated the brave's signal. When we turned back toward the buffalo, the Arapaho did the same, and our two groups speared in on either flank of the herd.

We were less than fifty yards from them when we came up on the animals. They singled out a fat cow, and one of the Indians rode in past it, steering it away from the herd. Another one rode right up alongside and dropped it with a shot.

"Let's try it," Will shouted, and kneed his mount. He ran in toward the herd, picked out a fat one, and cut it from the group, working it out toward us. When it was close I put a Hawken ball into its spine. Barney picked out another one and Will shot it. We had enough then and backed off between our kills to reload and wait.

The Indians added two more animals to their tally. Somewhere they had families to feed.

We worked on the kills one at a time, two men skinning and one standing guard, and the Indians across the draw from us did the same. As we finished the second animal, Pat Reasin and Lindy Moss came up with our extra horses. They held back at the top of the long slope until we waved them in.

When we had the hides and some meat packed we mounted up and headed north along the draw for a half mile or so, then drew rein to look back. The Arapaho were still there, dressing out their kill, and their main group had arrived. There were a dozen or more. As we turned, the brave who had given us the first signal raised an arm in salute, and I returned it. Then we rode far around them, bearing back to the west to camp that night a good five miles from the place.

"Another time," I told them that evening, "they might have had our scalps and horses. You just never know what an Indian is going to do."

"How did you know they wouldn't attack us today?" Shannon asked me.

"Because they said they wouldn't. I've not known one to lie."

We traveled together until the blue mountains were tall on the horizon; then I bid them farewell. They were turning southwest here; I was going straight on in.

"What will you do with your winter's catch, Randy?" McDowell asked, and I gave it thought before I answered.

"I'll buy horses," I told him. "And come next fall, I will take them to a place I know and begin a herd. The mountains will be filling up one day. Already there are settlers moving in. They'll need stock, and a man might make a living with a herd of horses and a tall-grass spread. Might even raise a family that way."

By calling to mind the landmarks I had first seen more than a year ago, I worked up the foothills for a week, then rode into the mountains along a little clear stream while early snow flecked the black's thickening coat and rimed my hat and my sleeves. I made camp for a couple of days in a stand of young spruce and bent trees to form a shelter frame while the storm blew itself out.

The weather was warming again when I crested a ridge where the little stream ran far below me, and looked down on a great sloping meadowland where the tall grass stood up through a mosaic of thin, crusted snow. The sight of it was like coming home.

I didn't try to find Billy LeCroix's grave, though I knew where it was. But I made a camp in that same grove where I had tarried long before helping a hurt Indian to heal, and when the first soft morning of brief Indian summer came upon me, I packed the horses, mounted the black, and headed upstream toward the cut from which I had first seen the great cathedral rock.

On the evening of the second day I came up through the heavy forest to the foot of mountains on the west side of the great rock and swung north. By last light I sat at the west gorge looking down into the hidden valley where so much had changed for me such a short time ago.

The rock stood there unaltered, just as I had seen it last, and the flat valley high with winter grass. Far away across its floor I could see dim forms of animals against the darkening snow.

I was halfway up the valley before my eyes could make out the shapes in the deepening gloom. I had expected elk—or buffalo. But they were horses, a good small herd of them, beginning to move back toward the sheltering cliff. And when I came around the outcrop, to where I could see the little cabin, there was a tendril of smoke rising from its top.

I had come home too late. Someone else had claimed the valley.

There was a figure by the corral as I walked the black toward it. I was almost there before I could make him out. An apparition stood there, leaning easy on a rail—an apparition in a great fur cloak, with a dead bear's face atop his head.

"Welcome home, Ran-Da-Hay," he said quietly. "I wondered when you'd get here."

Epilogue

Full spring was on the American section of Santa Fe. New lumber and fresh whitewash gleamed here and there in the golden afternoon sunlight, while vagrant breezes drifted the sounds of carpenters' hammers, a smith's ringing anvil, and muleskinners' curses.

Through the open double door of Patrick Fitzhugh O'Brien's warehouse strode an Indian. He lifted a spotless beaver tophat from his head and hung it on a peg, then swept back the great bearskin cape he wore to display a brilliance of brocaded vest over white linen shirt, gold-piped black vaquero pantaloons, and shiny boots.

A clerk at a counting table goggled. Fitz O'Brien looked up from his work and roared, "Han-Ra-Hay, by the Almighty!" He bustled forward to clasp hands with the Indian.

"I'm here to buy more horses and hardware, Fitz." The savage grinned. "We're going into the ranching business."

"We? Then Randall is with you?"

"Of course he is." The young redman's speech was closer to perfect English than was O'Brien's. "He made it back right on schedule. We picked up some good

206

hands, and we aim to raise horses up there by the big rock."

"So?" O'Brien beamed. "And he came down with you?"

"Sure, but he's gone courtin'. Brand new suit, collar fit to choke him to death, barbered 'til his ears stick out, and smelling to high heaven of bay rum." The Indian paused to flick a speck of dust from his linen sleeve.

"You know," he added, "it's a waste of money. That white-eyes really has no style."

VISIT THE WILD WEST
with Zebra Books

SPIRIT WARRIOR   (1795, $2.50)
by G. Clifton Wisler
The only settler to survive the savage Indian attack was a little boy. Although raised as a red man, every man was his enemy when the two worlds clashed—but he vowed no man would be his equal.

IRON HEART   (1736, $2.25)
by Walt Denver
Orphaned by an Indian raid, Ben vowed he'd never rest until he'd brought death to the Arapahoes. And it wasn't long before they came to fear the rider of vengeance they called . . . *Iron Heart*.

THE DEVIL'S BAND   (1903, $2.25)
by Robert McCaig
For Pinkerton detective Justin Lark, the next assignment was the most dangerous of his career. To save his beautiful young client's sisters and brother, he had to face the meanest collection of hardcases he had ever seen.

KANSAS BLOOD   (1775, $2.50)
by Jay Mitchell
The Barstow Gang put a bullet in Toby Markham, but they didn't kill him. And when the Barstow's threatened a young girl named Lonnie, Toby was finished with running and ready to start killing.

SAVAGE TRAIL   (1594, $2.25)
by James Persak
Bear Paw seemed like a harmless old Indian—until he stole the nine-year-old son of a wealthy rancher. In the weeks of brutal fighting the guns of the White Eyes would clash with the ancient power of the red man.